through to you

Also by Lauren Barnholdt

Watch Me
One Night That Changes Everything
Sometimes It Happens
The Thing About the Truth
Two-way Street
Right of Way

through to you

LAUREN BARNHOLDT

Simon Pulse

New York London Toronto Sydney New Delhi

SIMON PULSE

An imprint of Simon & Schuster Children's Publishing Division

1230 Avenue of the Americas, New York, New York 10020

This Simon Pulse paperback edition July 2015

Text copyright © 2014 by Lauren Barnholdt

Cover photograph copyright © 2014 by Jutta Klee/Corbis

Floral design copyright © 2014 by Thinkstock

Also available in a Simon Pulse hardcover edition.

For information about special discounts for bulk purchases, please contact Simon & Schuster Special Sales at 1-866-506-1949 or business@simonandschuster.com.

The Simon & Schuster Speakers Bureau can bring authors to your live event. For more information or to book an event contact the Simon & Schuster Speakers Bureau at 1-866-248-3049 or visit our website at www.simonspeakers.com.

Cover designed by Karina Granda

Interior designed by Hilary Zarycky

The text of this book was set in Cochin

Manufactured in the United States of America

2 4 6 8 10 9 7 5 3 1

The Library of Congress has cataloged the hardcover edition as follows:

Through to you / by Lauren Barnholdt. — 1st Simon Pulse hardcover ed.

p. cm.

Summary: When bad-boy Penn reaches out to cautious Harper, a tumultuous relationship blossoms, and the two learn that their bond may not be strong enough to overcome their obvious differences.

ISBN 978-1-4424-3463-9 (hc)

[1. Dating (Social customs) — Fiction. 2. Love — Fiction.] I. Title.

PZ7.B2667 Tj 2014

[Fic] — dc23

ISBN 978-1-4424-3464-6 (pbk)

ISBN 978-1-4424-3465-3 (ebook)

For my mom

ACKNOWLEDGMENTS

Thanks to all the usual suspects: Patrick Price, Alyssa Henkin, Kelsey Barnholdt, Krissi Barnholdt, Kevin Cregg, Stephanie Hoover, and everyone at S&S.

And Aaron, for everything, always.

The End

Harper

This is how it ends:

With me crying in a bathroom at the Crowne Plaza Hotel, cursing myself for being so stupid. I knew it was wrong, I knew it wasn't going to end well, I knew I was putting myself in a situation where I was going to end up brokenhearted.

I reach over and pull some toilet paper out of the dispenser and use it to blow my nose. My feet are killing me because of the stupid high heels I'm wearing. I want to sit down, but there's nowhere to sit. I'm in a bathroom stall, for God's sake. The only place to sit down is on the actual toilet, and it doesn't have a cover. Why don't the toilets in hotel bathrooms have covers? I'm sure I'm not the first person to end up in here crying her eyes out and looking for some privacy. Aren't there always scandalous things happening in hotels, things that would cause one to end up crying in the bathroom?

Okay, I tell myself, *just calm down. It's not as bad as you think.*

The problem, of course, is that it really *is* as bad as I think. I've never had my heart broken before, and I wasn't expecting it to feel like this. I wasn't expecting to feel like I want to die. I wasn't expecting to be crying so hard my shoulders shake and I can't breathe.

The door to the bathroom opens, and I hear footsteps crossing the floor. A group of girls laughing as they reapply their lipstick. They're happy and excited.

Like I should be.

But I'm not.

Instead, here I am.

Crying in a bathroom stall.

This is how it ends.

And I have no one to blame but myself.

I saw it coming.

I just couldn't stop it.

Penn

Harper isn't being fair.

I never wanted to break her heart.

She made the decision to break her own.

The Beginning

Harper

This is how it starts:

In world history, with a note, on a random Wednesday afternoon.

Penn Mattingly puts the note on my desk as he's walking to his seat in the back of the room.

Instantly I'm suspicious.

We're in high school. High school boys are notorious for leaving weird notes and other paraphernalia around, and usually whatever they've left doesn't say or represent anything nice or appropriate.

"What's that?" my best friend Anna says. Then she reaches across the aisle and plucks the note off my desk.

"Hey!" I don't know why, but suddenly I feel very protective of that note. I'm sure it says something totally ridiculous and/ or bordering on sexual harassment. One time sophomore year a senior left a note in Anna's locker that said, *I like your tits in that shirt.* If *I'd* gotten a note like that, I would have died. But Anna just smiled and took it as a compliment. And then she started dating that boy, which was kind of an unconventional way for a relationship to start. But whatever.

"What?" Anna asks as she starts to unfold the piece of paper. "We're best friends. We're supposed to share everything."

I reach over and steal it back. "I'll let you read it," I say, "but I should get to read it first."

But I don't open the paper, at least not right away. Instead I just hold it in my hand. In that second a shiver, almost like a premonition, runs up my spine. I feel like if I read what's on that piece of paper, I'm going to be starting down a road I can't turn back from.

"Open it!" Anna stage-whispers.

"Okay, okay." But still I don't. I turn around and glance back at Penn. He looks the same as always—shaggy dark hair that's just a little bit too long and flops over his forehead; broad shoulders; dark eyes. There's a little bit of stubble on his cheeks and chin, and he's wearing baggy jeans and a red hoodie.

He's joking around with Emmett Wilson and acting completely normal. I marvel at how different guys are from girls. How could Penn have left a note on my desk five seconds ago and now be pretending like it never happened? Meanwhile

Anna and I are sitting here making a huge deal about it before we've even read what it says.

"This is ridiculous," Anna says, rolling her eyes. She reaches out and grabs the note again.

I grab it back.

And then the bell rings and Mr. Marks walks in, and everyone faces front and gets quiet.

I spread the paper out on my lap.

It has one line on it, scrawled in boy handwriting.

I like your sparkle.

My hand reaches up and instinctively touches my hair, lingering on the piece of tinsel threaded through my ponytail. I didn't even want to wear the stupid tinsel, but it's senior spirit week, and Anna insisted we at least do *something*. So we met in the bathroom this morning and wove strands of tinsel through our hair. Green and blue, our school colors.

I didn't feel very sparkly at the time, but now, knowing Penn has noticed, my face feels all hot. I turn around and look at him again, but his eyes are on his notebook.

I catch Anna's eye and give her a disinterested shrug. Even though my heart is beating superfast, I have this weird feeling, like I shouldn't make a big deal of it to Anna.

So I mouth, "So stupid," and then pass her the note.

I know it's silly, but as soon as it's out of my hands, I want it back.

I'm not the kind of girl who gets notes like this from boys. No one has ever called me sparkly before.

Anna reads it, her eyebrows raised, then shrugs. "Kind of sweet?" she mouths.

She hands the note back to me, and then, suddenly, Mr. Marks turns his attention to us. "Something important, ladies?"

"What do you mean?" Anna asks in this half-snotty, half-fake-innocent voice. Anna's not scared of teachers. I'm scared of everything. Including, but not limited to: spiders, the dark, flying, and blood.

"I *mean* that you're passing notes in my class," Mr. Marks says. He holds his hand out. "Would you like to share it?"

My face burns.

"We weren't passing notes," Anna lies.

Mr. Marks's eyebrows knit together, and he glares at her. I guess what Anna's saying isn't technically a lie. *Technically* we weren't passing notes. At least not ones we'd written ourselves. Is Penn going to get in trouble too? I fight the urge to look back at him to see how he's reacting to this whole thing. I pretty much already know—the type of person to put a note on someone's desk that says *I like your sparkle* isn't the type to get all freaked out if they get in trouble for it.

The classroom phone buzzes on the wall.

Mr. Marks sighs and walks over to it.

"Yes," he says into the receiver. "Yes, she's here." His gaze turns to me, and I sit up straighter in my chair. Mr. Marks hangs up the phone and gives me a glare. "It seems you will be saved from my wrath for the time being, Ms. Fairbanks. You're wanted in the nurse's office."

Crap, crap, crap.

Anna gives me a sympathetic look as I gather up my books and leave the classroom. Once I'm in the hallway, I just stand there, not sure what to do. The period just started. Which means I'm going to have to wander the halls for the next forty-five minutes and hope I don't get caught.

Here's the deal with me and the nurse:

She's kind of stalking me.

I know that sounds crazy, but it's completely true. You'd think that someone who'd completed a bunch of medical training wouldn't have the capacity to be a stalker, but it just goes to show you that you can never tell what's lurking under the surface of someone's mind.

Okay, so maybe I'm being a little bit dramatic. The nurse isn't, like, restraining-order stalking me. It's just that there's some ridiculous rule that all seniors need to have a physical before graduation. It's, like, for some kind of state statistics or something, to make sure everyone's healthy. Most kids get them at their family doctors, or when they sign up for a sport. But one of my biggest fears is doctors and needles. So I haven't gone.

Unfortunately, if you don't show the school proof you've had one, they call you down to the nurse's office when the school doctor is in and try to give you one there. Um, no thank you. I've seen the school doctor. He has beefy fingers, and he smells like pepperoni and Swiss cheese. It's a ridiculous rule anyway. Why should the school get to dictate your, like, *health*?

I pull Penn's note back out from where I slipped it into my notebook and read it again.

I like your sparkle.

Was he being nice? Or is it one of those jerky things boys do just because they can? Was he making fun of me? I have no experience when it comes to this kind of thing. It's the first note I've received from a boy since the second grade, when Charles Dawcett put a note on my desk that asked me if I would be his girlfriend. I said yes, but by the time recess rolled around, he'd moved on to Addison Roach.

Whatever, I tell myself. *It's just a stupid note. It means nothing.*

But part of me can't help but wish it was something more.

And it's at that exact moment that Penn Mattingly appears behind me and tugs on a strand of my hair.

Penn

It was just a stupid note.

I wrote it on a whim, because I'd seen Harper walking into world history with that one friend she's always with, the one with the spiky hair. And Harper's tinsel sparkled in the light, and she reached up and smoothed her ponytail down, and something about the way she did it made it seem like she was wearing that tinsel ironically. I don't know why, but it was like she'd done it as an afterthought, like maybe someone had convinced her to wear it, like she couldn't even be bothered to wear a blue or green shirt for senior spirit week, so someone had to be like, "Hey, Harper, maybe you should wear this tinsel."

And that kind of killed me.

All these people walking around in their stupid school

spirit shirts, thinking that any of this means anything, and there she was wearing this tinsel in this completely ironic way.

So I ripped out a piece of paper from my notebook and wrote that I liked her sparkle. It was just a stupid note I dropped onto her desk. It wasn't supposed to *mean* anything.

But then I noticed she was looking back at me, and I kind of got a little bit nervous that maybe she *thought* it meant something more than it really did, so I pretended to be talking to the kid next to me.

And then I watched Mr. Marks catch her with the note, and I saw her fidget and get all uncomfortable, and in that moment, for some reason, I *wanted* him to read the note. Out loud. To the class. I hadn't signed my name, so no one would have known it was from me.

That's fucked up, I know. But I wanted Harper to be embarrassed. Actually, no, that's not completely true. I didn't want her embarrassed, per se. I just wanted to have an effect on her. I *liked* that I was having an effect on her.

So when she got called down to the nurse's office, I immediately jumped up and asked for the bathroom pass.

I thought I'd have to go running around looking for her, but she was just standing there in the hallway, looking down at something. When I got closer, I saw she was reading my note.

A feeling of trepidation came over me. Why was she reading my note again? Maybe she was a stalker. I sized her up. Long dark hair, average height, wearing jeans and a pink tank top with a sheer white shirt over it.

She didn't look like a stalker. And besides, I was the one who'd put a note on her desk. If anything, *I* was the one who could be considered a stalker.

But still.

You can never tell. What do stalkers really look like? You'd expect them to be girls who aren't all that cute, girls who are desperate for male attention. But from my experience— and honestly, not to sound like an asshole, but I have kind of a lot of it—the ones you need to worry about are the ones who *are* good-looking. It's like they're so used to getting what they want, they can't take no for an answer.

Is Harper good-looking? I wasn't sure yet.

"Whatcha doin'?" I ask, and lightly pull on a strand of her hair.

She turns around, startled, and drops the note I gave her.

We both bend down to pick it up, and then we both stop when we see what the other one is doing, and so we end up just kind of crouched down over the floor together. I stay like that for a moment longer than necessary, because I can tell she's flustered. I know it's fucked up, but like I said, I like that I'm having an effect on her. Finally she grabs the note and we both stand up.

"Um, I'm not doing anything." She smoothes her ponytail, and her tinsel shimmers. "What are you doing?"

I shrug. "Why do you have to go to the nurse?" I ask. "Are you sick?" She doesn't look sick.

"I'm not going to the nurse." A look of panic crosses her face.

17

"But you just got called down."

"So?"

"So then why aren't you going?" It's almost funny, me asking someone why they're not doing something. I never do anything I'm supposed to.

She shrugs and shifts her weight from foot to foot. "I don't know."

"Liar."

"Whatever." She pushes her hair back from her face and looks at me defiantly, like she's waiting for me to say something. So I don't.

"Okay, well. I guess I'm just going to go walk around," she says finally.

"The *school*?"

"Yeah."

"Why?"

"Because I just told you, I'm not going to the nurse."

I have no idea what she's talking about. She definitely might be a crazy person. Not, like, a dangerous crazy person or anything. Although, usually if people are nuts in one way, they have the potential to be nuts in all sorts of other ways. But I kind of like it. I like that she's always been quiet in world history, and now here she is, talking nonsense.

"What do you have against nurses?" I tease. I start walking down the hall, just in case Mr. Marks decides to come out and make sure I'm actually going to the bathroom.

Harper follows me.

"Nothing, really."

"Well, you must have *something* against them." Is it possible she doesn't know the amazingness that is the nurse's office? "You know if you go down there and tell them you threw up in the bathroom, they'll let you go home. It's, like, a rule."

"She wants me to have a physical," Harper says, "and I have a phobia."

"Of physicals?"

"Of all things medical." She looks at me and raises her chin, challenging me to call her crazy. But I don't. A girl who can admit what she's afraid of is refreshing.

"It's just a school physical, though. You know that, right? They don't take blood or anything." It's true. I've had a million sports physicals for baseball, and if you're not, like, five minutes away from dying or have scoliosis, the physicals are totally useless.

She shrugs. "It's all the same to me."

I'm still walking down the hall, and she's still following me. "So you're just gonna wander around the school?"

She nods. "Until the end of the period, yeah. Then hopefully they'll have forgotten they want to see me."

What a horrible plan. Everyone knows that if you're trying to get away with skipping class, you don't hang around at *school*. "That's the worst idea ever," I tell her. "Someone's going to catch you."

"No, they won't," she says. "I'm going to hide in the bathroom."

"Oh my God," I say, rolling my eyes. "That's the first place they look!" It's such an innocent, ridiculous plan that I can't help think that maybe she's joking. But there's no sign of a smile on her face. I shake my head and then look her up and down. She bites her lip, and she looks so damn cute and kind of like a lost puppy that I can't resist. "You wanna get out of here?"

She looks shocked. "Leave the school?"

"Yeah."

"With *you*?"

"Yes."

"And do *what*?"

"I don't know. Eat. Walk. Have an adventure." I give her my patented smile, the one I use when I want to get my way.

She taps her foot against the floor. "I don't even know you."

"Penn Mattingly." I put my hand out, and she gives me a look like she can't believe I'm trying to pull bullshit on her.

"I know your name."

"So what else do you need?" I pull my wallet out and hand her my license. "Name, date of birth, address . . ."

She looks down at it doubtfully. "That's a horrible picture of you."

"Really?" I cock my head. "I kind of like it. It was after this crazy party, and this girl had . . ." I trail off for a moment, then reach out and take the license back. "Well. It was just a rough night. So given the circumstances, I think I look pretty good."

"Are you always this cocky?"

I shake my head and pretend like she's got me all wrong. "It's a real shame," I tell her, "that you would think that about me."

"You just told me you think you look good in that picture, and that you had some kind of random sexual escapade with a girl. What else am I supposed to think? I mean, I haven't ever spoken to you until today. You're not exactly making the best first impression." She turns on her heel and starts walking away from me.

I chase after her, wondering how I've suddenly become the follower instead of the followee. "That's awful," I say. "That we've been in the same school all this time and we've never even talked. I mean, what if we're soul mates?"

She turns on her heel and gapes at me. "Me and *you*?"

"What, like you're too good for me?"

She shrugs, like maybe she thinks she is. I'm annoyed for a second, and then I realize she's probably right. I might have never spoken to her until today, but I know she's smart. I know she's quiet. I know she always eats lunch outside when the weather is nice. All those things make her too good for me, because the truth is, pretty much any girl who has her shit together is too good for me.

But I push that thought out of my head as best I can, because if I let myself think about that, I won't be able to convince her to come with me. And I don't know why, but I really, really want her to.

21

"Anyway," I say. "Now that we've explored that possibility, we really shouldn't waste another moment. Let's get out of here."

She tugs on her hair again, and I can see her mind working. She *wants* to go with me, but she's a good girl. Her instinct is probably to be afraid and cautious. *My* instinct is to give her another grin and make a witty comment, but some part of me has a feeling that's not going to work.

So I just wait.

And sure enough, after a moment Harper shrugs. "Okay," she says. "Let's go."

Harper

Oh my God.

This is crazy.

This might be the craziest thing I've ever done. Which really isn't saying that much. I mean, I don't do crazy things, like, ever. Although, sometimes, if someone is making me feel like I'm too chicken to do something, I get kind of mad and then I do it.

Like the time last summer when everyone at my dance camp was jumping off this rope swing at the lake, and I was totally afraid to do it because every time someone used that rope, all I could think about was them falling and smashing their heads open. People in books and movies are always getting killed when they jump off rope swings. Always.

It's, like, a thing. And every time I watched a movie or read a book like that, I'd always be like, who would be stupid enough to jump off a rope swing? But then there I was, and everyone was doing it, and so then I kind of had to.

It wasn't because everyone was making fun of me. It was because no one was making fun of me. It was like no one expected me to do it, so much so that they didn't even bother to try to make me feel lame for not doing it. Which pissed me off.

So I did it. I didn't crack my head open, but I did almost lose my bathing suit top.

But this.

Leaving school in the middle of the day? I've never done that.

Leaving school in the middle of the day with a boy? I've *definitely* never done that.

Leaving school in the middle of the day with a boy who looks that good in his driver's license picture and knows it? A whole new definition of "outside the realm of possibility."

Not to mention he's a *strange* boy.

Not like "strange" in the sense of being weird. "Strange" like he's a stranger. I glance at him out of the corner of my eye, wondering if he's psycho. I run through a list of things in my head that I know about Penn Mattingly.

1. He has an I-don't-care attitude.
2. He used to be a big baseball star, before he hurt his shoulder or something last year.

3. He gets away with murder, I think mostly because of his I-don't-care attitude. Like, for example, if he comes into class late, the teachers hardly bother saying anything to him about it, because he doesn't give a shit. There's nothing you can really do to him, because he doesn't care if he ends up in the office.

4. He's hot. This is a new one to the list. I mean, I always knew Penn was good-looking. But it was more something I noticed abstractly, not something I was necessarily super-aware of. But now I am. Super-aware of it, I mean. I'm super-aware of the way his hair flops over his forehead, how smooth his skin is, how broad his shoulders are, and how he towers over me, even though I'm five-eight.

"Where are we going?" I ask as we walk through the front doors of the school. As soon as we're outside, I have to resist the urge to look over my shoulder and make sure no one has seen us. Penn, on the other hand, is walking like he doesn't have a care in the world.

He glances back at me and gives me this totally mischievous grin. "Stop asking me that. I told you I don't know."

"Yeah, but how can you not know? I mean, shouldn't we have a plan or something?"

"Plans are for wimps."

I don't want to seem like a wimp, so I just follow him. He's walking with a crazy confidence, like we're totally justified in leaving school in the middle of the morning, and not just two delinquents who are skipping class. I wonder how many times he's done this, and if he's somehow perfected the casual I'm-supposed-to-be-doing-this walk. I try to mimic it and almost trip over my feet.

I'm still not sure if I'm going to actually go anywhere with him. Leaving school is one thing, but leaving school *property* is another.

As soon as I see his car, my mind gets made up.

"*That's* your car?" I ask as he unlocks the passenger-side door for me.

"Yeah." He opens the door and motions for me to get inside.

I shake my head. "No way. I'm not getting in there."

"Why not?"

"Because, it's . . ." I try to think of a way to put it delicately. I know how boys can be about their cars, and I don't think he'll like it too much if I tell him it looks like a death trap. But it does. It's not that it's run-down or anything. In fact, it's the opposite. It's shiny and black and looks really new. But it's a truck, and it's one of those trucks that have double wheels or whatever.

Double wheels that look dangerous, like the kind of thing you use to street race, or whatever it is teenage boys do when their hormones are raging and they're bored. A truck like that cannot be trusted. A *boy* who has a truck like that cannot be trusted.

"It's what?" Penn asks impatiently.

The sun is starting to move higher in the sky, and it's a

lot hotter out here than it was inside. Penn unzips his hoodie, then takes it off and tosses it into the backseat. His arms are strong and lean, and his biceps flex under the thin material of his white T-shirt as he opens the door of his truck wider, inviting me in.

I quickly look away and force myself to ignore the buzz that's starting to vibrate through my body.

"It doesn't look . . . I mean, it looks . . ."

He rolls his eyes. "I'm a very good driver."

"You are?"

He nods solemnly. "Of course. You really think my parents would let me drive a car like this if I was reckless?" He puffs his chest proudly. "I've only been in three accidents."

Oh, for the love of . . . I turn around and start to head back toward the school, but he reaches out and grabs my arm. "I'm kidding, I'm kidding," he says. "I've never been in an accident."

"Ever?"

"Ever. And I passed my driver's test on my first try, I swear."

I swallow. I'm not sure if he's telling the truth. He seems like the kind of guy who could lie and make it seem completely true. He also seems like he's used to getting what he wants. Both of those things are having conflicting effects on me. On one hand, it's making me not want to go with him, but on the other hand, it's making me *want* to go with him. The whole thing is very weird.

"Come on," he says. "If we don't hurry, someone's going

to find us out here, and then you're going to have more than getting into my truck to worry about."

He's right.

And besides, I want to go.

So I climb into the front seat.

Penn

Usually when I have a girl in my truck, we just drive around until I find a random spot for us to park in and make out. Either that or we end up at some party where we get drunk and then end up making out. Wow. I never realized how often I end up making out with girls. Pretty much every time I'm hanging out with one.

I'm not sure if I should be proud of this. Probably not.

Anyway. Obviously I can't do this with Harper. I glance at her out of the corner of my eye. Even if I want to.

"So, any idea where you're taking me?" Harper asks. She's trying to sound nonchalant, but I can tell she's suspicious. I don't even know her, and she's acting like I'm bad news. I mean, I *am* bad news. But there's no way she can know that yet.

"Why are you so suspicious of me?" I ask.

"Because you left a note on my desk and now you're whisking me away somewhere." She reaches over and opens my glove compartment.

"Whisking you away? Is that what you think I'm doing?" Something about me whisking her away makes me happy. It sounds almost whimsical.

"Yeah. You coerced me into this truck, and now you're whisking me." She pulls a bunch of stuff out of the glove compartment— papers, a pair of sunglasses, some napkins—and starts looking through them. I'm not sure if I should be angry or impressed.

"I didn't *coerce* you anywhere," I say. "You came here of your own volition. And stop going through my stuff."

She ignores my request and raises her eyebrows at me. "Wow," she says. "'Volition.' Big word."

"You think I don't know words like 'volition'?"

"I don't know if you do," she says. "I don't know anything about you." She holds up a receipt that was buried in my glove compartment. "Wow, except that you spent two hundred and thirty-two dollars at Hooters."

"*What?* Let me see that." I reach over and grab the receipt out of her hand.

"Yeah, and only twenty dollars for a tip." She clucks her tongue. "Less than ten percent. That's awful, Penn. Those girls work hard for their tips."

"That's not mine," I say.

She raises her eyebrows and gives a skeptical little laugh.

"It isn't! My friend Jackson used to borrow my truck whenever he'd want to get up to something. He was dating this girl who was supercr— Um, didn't like what . . . He just needed to borrow my truck when he wanted chicken wings."

"Mmm," she says noncommittally. "Sounds like a lie."

"It's actually not." Figures that one of the only times I'm telling the truth, I don't even get credit for it. I hit my blinker and head east. I have no idea where we're going and what we're going to do, so I just drive.

Harper doesn't say anything. She just puts my stuff back into the glove compartment (*shoves* my stuff back into the glove compartment, is more like it), then nonchalantly reaches into her purse and pulls out her phone. She starts to text someone.

"Who are you texting?" I ask, mostly just to make conversation.

"None of your business." She moves her phone away from me.

I sigh. "Seriously? It's going to be like that?"

"Like what?"

"Like every time I ask you something, you're going to make a big point of showing me just how much you don't trust me."

"Trust needs to be earned," she reports.

"Apparently not," I say. "Since you just got into my truck with me, no questions asked."

"I asked questions!"

"Hardly."

She's still texting, and I catch a glimpse of the words . . . *in his truck. If he kills me, then* . . .

I reach over and grab the phone out of her hand. "Hey!" she says.

We roll to a stop at a red light, and I glance down at the screen. "Anna," I read out loud. "Is that the girl with the spiky hair you're always with?"

She nods. "What are you, like a stalker?"

"Please," I say. "You guys are always together. It's impossible not to notice."

She grabs for the phone, and I give it back to her. "I'm glad you're telling your friend that we're going somewhere," I say. "I think it's a good idea."

"You do?"

"Yeah. That way you won't be able to deny you were with me."

"Why would I deny I was with you?"

"Because we're skipping class right now, and if we get caught, you're probably going to try to say we weren't together."

"That makes no sense." She shakes her head and then looks back down at the screen. It seems like her friend has texted her back. She frowns.

"Let me guess," I say. "She's telling you to come back to school right this instant."

"No," Harper says. "She told me that you're the kind of guy I could get into a lot of trouble with."

I glance at her out of the corner of my eye. I wonder if she's the kind of girl I want to get into trouble with. I've made up my mind. Harper is definitely hot. "I don't even know this Anna," I say. "But already I can tell she's smart."

Harper

The way Penn's looking at me, like maybe he wants to kiss me or maybe even get me naked, is making butterflies swarm around in my stomach. He's just so . . . I don't know, *real*.

Like, what guy do you know who admits he's trouble? Although, the fact that he's admitting he's trouble is definitely a big red flag. It's like a huge, huge, huge red flag. I'm not sure if I should be glad he's being honest, or nervous that he's obviously crazy enough to think that admitting how much trouble you are is okay.

I'm not the kind of girl who looks for trouble. I'm not even the kind of girl who finds trouble when she's *not* looking for it.

"Where are you taking me?" I ask. I think it's a good variation of my usual "Where are we going?"

"God, you really are uptight, aren't you?" Penn asks. He shifts the truck into another gear, and as he does, his hand brushes against my thigh. I'm not sure if it's my imagination, but I feel like maybe he did it on purpose.

"No." I don't think I'm uptight. Am I uptight? I don't think I am. But probably people who are uptight don't realize they're uptight. Oh God. I might be uptight. "I'm just not used to strange boys accosting me in the hallway."

He grins. "I'm a man."

I snort.

"And I'm sick of you being so suspicious of me."

"You haven't known me long enough to be sick of anything about me."

"I've known you long enough." He looks over at me, and his gaze slides up my body. Suddenly I feel kind of exposed and uncomfortable, and I shift on the seat, intentionally moving my leg away just in case his hand goes for the gearshift again.

"You've known me for all of ten minutes."

"So then tell me something about yourself."

I reel off the list of things I always keep on hand for these situations—like when they ask you to name three things about yourself at the beginning of camp or on the first day of school or something. (Which is so stupid. Who remembers anything from the first day of school?) "My middle name's Louise, I'm an only child, I want to be a choreographer, and my best subject is math."

"Your best subject is world history, because I'm in it. And those things you just told me are lame."

"They are not lame!"

"Yes, they are. They don't tell me anything about you." Penn shakes his head and then looks at me before returning his gaze to the road. "Tell me something good."

I don't know what he means. Those things I told him *are* good. Especially about me wanting to be a choreographer. People are always super-impressed with that one. And my middle name being Louise? That's a hideous middle name.

I look down and try to think of something scandalous I can tell him. The floor of Penn's truck is littered with straw wrappers, but other than that it's sparkling clean.

"I'm going to Ballard," I say. "You know, the music school? I've already been accepted to the school, I just have to audition for the choreography program."

He shrugs, like he's never heard of it, even though it's, like, one of the most prestigious schools in the country. Then he sort of shakes his head, like he should have known better than to ask me to tell him something scandalous.

Which pisses me off.

I can be scandalous.

Can't I?

"My dad cheated on my mom when I was four months old, and he took off and I haven't heard from him since."

Penn cocks his head, like he's maybe a little bit interested.

"And one time I overheard my mom saying I would probably have issues with men because of it."

"And do you?"

"Have issues with men?"

"Yes."

"Well, I'm not sure. I don't know any men."

He smiles.

He opens his mouth to ask me something else, but suddenly I don't want him to. I realize it's because I'm intimidated by him. Penn is beautiful and interesting and charming, and the only thing I have to offer is an absent father and a dance audition.

I check the clock. "We should probably go back to school," I say. "The period's almost over."

Penn looks at me in shock. "You want to go back to *school*?"

"Well, yeah." It's one thing to get away with skipping world history. Probably no one would catch me, since I was technically supposed to be in the nurse's office anyway. It's another thing altogether to end up missing a whole day. No way I would be able to get away with that.

He shakes his head. "You obviously haven't had much practice at this."

He's right, but I don't want him to know that, so I just roll my eyes.

After a moment he turns the car around. "Okay, fine," he says. "I'll take you back to school."

As soon as he turns around, I want to take it back. I realize that once we're back at school, we'll be away from each other. And it's weird, but I don't want to leave him. I don't know anything about him, and yet I don't want to be away from him. It's a very unsettling feeling.

When we get back to school, he pulls into a parking spot near the front. He stops the car but leaves it idling.

"Aren't you coming in?" I ask, surprised.

"Nah," he says. "The point of walking out of school when you're not supposed to is that you stay out for the whole day."

"Okay." I get out of the car. "Well, um . . ." I'm not sure what to say. Thanks for the ride? See you soon?

"Have a good day," is what comes out. *Have a good day.* Ridiculous. Silly. Mortifying.

Penn just smiles. "Have a good day, Harper Fairbanks," he says.

I shut the door.

And Penn pulls away, leaving me standing there with butterflies swarming around in my stomach.

Penn

I pull out of the parking lot, leaving Harper standing in front of the school, and in that moment I decide I need to stay away from her. She's definitely not the kind of girl I need to be getting involved with. Actually, strike that. I don't need to be getting involved with any girl, not now, not ever.

At least not in the sense of having an actual relationship. I'm bad at relationships. Not that I've ever had a relationship—at least, not in a romantic sense. But the rest of my relationships are pretty much all fucked up, so it's not a stretch to believe that I might be bad at the romantic ones too.

As if to illustrate this point, at that moment my phone rings. It's my older brother, Braden.

"Hello?" I answer, trying to keep my voice light. There's only one reason Braden would be calling me during the day, only one reason he'd be bothering me. (I'd like to say he doesn't call me during the day because he knows I'm in school and doesn't want to take me away from my studies, but that's definitely not true. Braden couldn't give two shits about school, illustrated by the fact that he barely graduated high school and then dropped out of community college halfway through his first semester.)

"Oh, hi," he says, like he's surprised that I answered. I can picture him on the other end of the line, clutching his phone in his hand and chewing his lip. Even though Braden is two years older than me, he's pretty much useless. At least when it comes to what I know he's about to tell me.

"Braden," I say, forcing faux cheer into my voice. "To what do I owe the honor of this phone call?"

"It's Dad," he says. "Uh, he left."

"Really?" I try to sound fake shocked. It's a little game I like to play with myself, almost like I'm an actor on a soap opera and it's my job to have the craziest, most over-the-top reactions that I can. You'd be surprised how easy it actually is.

"Penn," Braden says. "He really did leave."

Braden has no sense of humor. Either that or he's trying to one-up me by pretending he doesn't know what I'm doing. But I'll bet the former.

"Okay." I shrug, even though he can't see me. "Any idea where he went?" It's a rhetorical question. No one knows where my dad goes when he disappears, except that we can all be sure that wherever it is, there's a bar.

"No."

"Then there's nothing I can do."

I hear a flipping sound on the other end of the line, probably Braden peeking through the blinds, like maybe he's going to be able to spot my dad's car somewhere, or get some clue as to where he's gone.

"But what if . . . Penn, he could hurt someone."

"I know," I say. It's the only thing that still bothers me, the only thing that makes me nervous about my dad and his little trips. If he wants to go out driving drunk and kill himself, that's one thing. Hurting someone else—well, that's different. But if it's going to happen, there's nothing I can do about it. In fact, I learned a long time ago that there's nothing you can do about most of the bad things that are going to happen in life.

"Okay, well . . ." Braden says.

I wait for him to finish his thought, but he doesn't.

"I'll be home later," I say. "I have some stuff to do after school."

"Okay." Braden doesn't ask questions. I'm lying to him, obviously. One, I'm not even at school. And two, I hadn't even decided until just now that I'm going to stay out. But now that my dad is gone, I know what the vibe of my house is going to be like—tense and depressing.

"See you then," I say.

"Yeah."

Braden hangs up. We're not much for goodbyes in my family.

Harper

When I get back to school, the period isn't over yet, and so everything is all deserted. Well, not *deserted* deserted. There are still people here, obviously.

I can hear muted voices drifting out of classrooms and into the hallway. But there's no one around. I head to my locker, figuring that if anyone asks me what I'm doing, I can always say I'm coming back from the nurse's office. I doubt anyone's going to check, especially since I'm not the kind of person who gets in trouble. I look very responsible, especially with this tinsel in my hair.

Yes, I might have worn it under protest, but now that I have it in, it shows that I'm totally into school spirit.

But it turns out I don't even have to worry about it, because by the time I get to my locker, I haven't seen one teacher. In fact, the only person I've passed is a freshman girl who's walking down the hall, crying, her black eyeliner smudged under her eyes.

I think about asking her what's wrong, but she glares at me, and so I look away. She can't be in that bad a state if she's able to glare like that. And honestly, it's not that weird to see someone walking down the hall crying. It's one of those crazy things about high school. Things that would seem out of place in the world are completely normal here.

When I get to my locker, I pull out the books I'm going to need for the rest of the day. There's an energy zooming through my body, and I think it's because of Penn. Which is crazy. There's nothing going on between me and Penn.

But he left you a note. He put a note on your desk that said he liked your sparkle. Why did he do that? *Maybe he likes you.* The thought is delicious, and it sends a flicker of nervousness and excitement over my skin.

I'm surprised to find that my heart is beating fast.

Stop, I tell myself. *He's just a stupid boy.*

I keep repeating it to myself, like if I say it enough times, I'll believe it. Which is kind of ridiculous, because I already do believe it. He is a stupid boy. It shouldn't take any convincing.

The bell rings then, and kids come pouring out of the classrooms and into the hallway, which immediately becomes filled with talking and laughter and screaming and yelling.

I shut my locker and start walking toward my next class.

It feels disorienting to be out here like this, in between classes, without having actually come from another class.

So disorienting that I realize I'm heading the wrong way.

I'm too embarrassed to do an about-face in the middle of the hall, so I have to go around the long way.

This is not about Penn Mattingly, I tell myself.

And for the rest of the day, whenever he pops into my head, I just keep repeating the same thing.

He's just a stupid boy.

He's just a stupid boy.

He's just a stupid boy.

Anna, however, doesn't want to let me forget him.

"I cannot *believe* you left school with him!" she yells at the end of the day. She's standing in front of the cafeteria doors, which is where we always meet after the last bell. Anna and I drive to school together every day, and leave together every day. There aren't enough parking spots for everyone, so the school institutes a lottery system at the beginning of each year. We both put our names in and said that if only one of us got a spot, we would share it. Anna got a spot, and I didn't, and so each day we take turns driving. So far it's worked out perfectly.

"I didn't, like, *leave* school with him," I say, even though I totally did. I mean, there's no real way to spin it. "And be quiet."

I look around furtively, hoping no one's able to overhear

us. The last thing I need is the rumor mill starting up that me and Penn Mattingly are, like, a thing. Not that I've ever been part of the rumor mill. And not like anyone probably cares or even knows what Anna is talking about.

"I *am* being quiet," Anna says, even though she's not being quiet at all. She pumps money into the machine against the wall that dispenses tea, hot chocolate, and coffee. Technically only teachers are supposed to use it, but if you do it after school, no one will really give you a hard time.

Anna pushes the button for a hot green tea, and the machine roars to life.

"I don't know how you can drink that stuff," I say, shaking my head. Green tea is disgusting, and she drinks it without any sugar or milk or anything. But Anna's a singer, and so she never drinks anything except hot drinks. Even when she's just drinking water, she heats it up and puts lemon in it.

"I have to," Anna says. "My throat is completely raw. And stop trying to change the subject."

"I'm not," I say, even though I am. "There's no subject to even really talk about."

"Your face is getting red and your voice is getting all wobbly," Anna reports.

"No, it isn't."

"Yes, it is."

We push through the front doors of the school and start heading for Anna's car. The weather is nice, warm with a slight breeze. But in the distance I can see storm clouds, and I hope it isn't going to rain. I hate the rain. It always puts me in a bad mood.

"So where'd you guys go, anyway?" Anna asks.

I think about the question. Something tells me, "We drove around and talked about nothing" isn't really going to go over that well. "Just . . . you know . . . around."

"Why are you being so vague?" she asks. We're at her car now, and I wait for her to unlock the doors, but she doesn't. Instead she just plops her bag down onto the car, then sets her green tea down next to it.

Then she hops up onto the hood.

"What are you doing?" I say, even though I already know.

"You know exactly what I'm doing. Car Talk."

Car Talks are something Anna and I came up with when we were ten, right before her parents told her they were getting divorced. They were fighting a lot, and Anna didn't like being in the house when they really got going. So she'd head outside and climb into her dad's car.

I'd look out my bedroom window and wait until I saw her, then creep downstairs and fill a brown paper lunch sack with apple slices and peanut butter (our favorite) before sneaking outside. We'd sit in the car and talk and eat. We didn't necessarily talk about her parents arguing, although sometimes we did. A lot of times we'd just talk about what boys we thought were cute, or what teachers were fair and which ones weren't.

And even though after her parents got divorced Anna moved and doesn't live across the street from me anymore, now

45

anytime we talk about something important, we do it in the car.

"We don't have Car Talks on the hood," I grumble now.

"Well, we should." Anna reaches around and pushes her hair up off her neck. "It's too hot to sit in the car."

"If you'd get your air conditioning fixed, we wouldn't have that problem." I launch myself up onto the hood and sit down next to her.

"You know I don't have the money for that." She takes another sip of her green tea. "My final Juilliard audition is coming up soon, and I have lessons with Sam every day next week."

Sam is Anna's voice coach. He's supposedly brilliant, and he costs some exorbitant amount of money per lesson, which Anna has to pay for with what she earns working at the pretzel place in the mall.

"Oh, that's good," I say. "What are you guys working on?" She doesn't answer right away, and so I babble on. "I'm working on my audition piece for Ballard. I mean, of course it's almost done. But I need to make sure it's perfect, you know?"

She shakes her head. "No way. We're not talking about colleges. Tell me about Penn."

"Would you get over this whole Penn thing?" I roll my eyes. "There's nothing to tell!"

"Then why did he give you a note saying that he likes your sparkle?" She throws a hand over her mouth and then jumps off the hood of the car. "Ohmigod! If you guys get married, it will be all because of me!"

"No one's getting married." I'm not sure Penn's really even boyfriend material. That truck of his definitely doesn't scream "dependable."

"Well, even if you have a great love with him, then it will be because of me." She gives me a pointed look. "Just think, if you hadn't been wearing that tinsel this morning. . . ." She twirls around in a circle.

"Yeah," I say, getting down and heading for the passenger side. "And if it turns out horribly, that will be all your fault too."

Fifteen minutes later Anna drops me off in front of my mom's dance studio, where I work almost every day after school.

Here's what you need to know about my work:

1. I'm the receptionist and manager, which basically means I'm in charge of scheduling everyone's lessons. This isn't that fun a job, but it's not that bad, either.
2. My mom wants me to be a dance teacher like her, and so she's always trying to get me to teach. But the thing is, I don't want to be a teacher. Even though I've been dancing ever since I was little, I've always wanted to choreograph. I love to dance, but I don't have the right body type to be a career dancer, and even if I did, I'm not sure I'd want to put myself through a dancer's disciplined life. Teaching is fine, but I'd rather be choreographing than teaching people basic moves.

3. My mom's studio focuses on ballroom dance. I can rumba and salsa, but I'm not that good at it. I know the basic steps, but I don't have the magic that a lot of ballroom dancers have, where they just sail across the floor like it's nothing. I like hip-hop, or freestyle, even though you'd never know it by looking at me. But when I hear that kind of music, it's like my brain clicks into another gear. I start imagining different moves, different ways for the beats to fit together to create a whole.

Inside the studio my mom's working with a young couple on a first dance for their wedding. The girl has long dark hair, and she looks like she's about to kill her fiancé.

"That's not how you do it, Jeremy," the bride-to-be says. She takes a deep breath and then blows her bangs out of her face. "She said it's quick-quick-slow for the steps, not quick-quick-quick!" She throws her arms around him and then starts sort of dragging him around the dance floor. It's actually funny, because even though she was the one who was yelling, he's a better dancer than her. The girl is trying way too hard. She holds her arms back and her shoulders all stiff. If you're not a real ballroom dancer, you look really stupid doing that.

"Wonderful," my mom says, obviously deciding to go for the encouraging approach. "Yes, that's it!"

The two of them plod around the dance floor until the girl steps on the guy's foot. He doubles over in pain. "Ow! Ow!" he yells. "Jesus, Kaitlyn, are you trying to kill me?"

"No," she mutters. "But God knows I want to."

I give my mom a quick wave and then head to the office, happy my mom is occupied, but feeling bad that she's dealing with a wedding dance. My mom hates having to teach lessons for a couple's wedding dance. Usually the people are completely hopeless, because they've never danced before in their lives. All they do is fight the whole time, and once they're done with their dance, they never buy any more lessons. Usually my mom foists them off on one of the younger teachers, but it looks like Sheila and Michael are in the back ballroom, probably dealing with other students.

I sit down at my desk and do what I always do when I get into work—pull up the internet. I log on to Facebook, and Anna immediately chats me from her phone.

Let's have a party! she declares.

We don't know enough people to have a party, I type back. Not to mention we're not the party types. We hardly ever go to parties, and when we do, we end up standing in the corner, talking only to each other, which kind of defeats the purpose of going to a party.

We don't have to know people, she replies. *People will come to a party if there's free booze.*

And where are we going to get money for booze? I ask. *Or someone to buy it for us?*

Details, details, comes the reply.

I roll my eyes.

We have nothing to celebrate, I remind her. *Our birthdays already passed.*

49

We could have a "we're so awesome" party.

I admire her positive attitude, but I seriously do hate parties. I'm not even into birthdays the way some girls are. I couldn't care less about getting another year older. Yeah, it's nice to have cake and get presents, but I'm not all, "Look at me, look at me" like Kinsey Harlow, who wears a pink tiara on her birthday every year, and makes all her friends buy her flowers. Well, I don't know that she *makes* them. But it's definitely, like, expected.

I'm about to tell Anna she's crazy, when the phone rings, so I type a quick *brb.*

The studio technically opens at one o'clock for lessons, but those have to be scheduled. The actual walk-in hours start at three, so those are the hours we have listed on our website. Which means that at three the phone starts ringing off the hook.

"Good afternoon. Dance On," I say in my happiest voice. There's no answer.

"Good afternoon. Dance On," I repeat, louder this time. A lot of our dance clients are elderly, and so they have a hard time hearing.

"Jesus," a voice says. "Why are you screaming?"

"I'm not *screaming,*" I say. "I thought maybe you were having trouble hearing me."

"Who could have trouble hearing you when you're talking so loud? You almost blew my eardrums out."

I take a deep breath and remember that the customer is

always right. Well, except when they're trying to cancel their lessons without twenty-four hours notice and expect to get their money back. "I'm sorry," I say. "Can I help you? Would you like to schedule a lesson?"

"That depends," the male voice says, his tone getting all low. "Will you be teaching it?"

"No, I'm not a teacher."

"Then no."

"No?"

"No. I only want a lesson from you." The tone is flirty now. And strangely familiar.

"Who is this?" I demand. I picture Anna putting someone from school up to this. I wonder if it's her older brother, Gregory. Gregory's a lot older than us, but he's money hungry. He'd definitely do it for a few bucks. Although, I don't know why Anna would want to prank me. She's not usually the type to—

"It's Penn."

My throat goes dry at the sound of his name. "Oh." I grasp around in my brain for something else to say. Why is he calling me? "Why are you calling me?" I blurt.

"Wow," he says. "Way to make me feel welcome."

"Sorry," I say. "It's just . . . How did you know I work here?"

"It's on your Facebook page."

"You were on my Facebook page?" It's a weird feeling, a guy telling me he was on my Facebook page. I hope Anna untagged me from that photo she took of us at the beach last summer. I have tan marks from my sunglasses, and the gauzy cover-up I was wearing blew up in the breeze, making me look like I was pregnant.

"Yeah. So?" He sounds defensive.

"No reason."

There's a pause. "So can I have a lesson or what?"

"Um, I . . ." I'm confused. Is he really calling for a lesson?

"I'm kidding," he says. "I don't want a lesson. Like I said, unless you're teaching it." His voice is even more flirty and husky now, and my face burns. My heart's beating fast, and I'm not sure if it's because of the fact that he's all kinds of sexy right now or because I'm starting to realize that I might be blowing it with him. How come I don't have any witty comebacks? I should be able to do this. I should be able to converse with him.

"Sorry, I'm not a teacher." Definitely not a witty comeback, but also definitely better than dead silence.

"And you can't make an exception?"

"Why do you want to learn to dance anyway?"

"I don't."

I sigh. "Then why are you calling to get a dance lesson?"

"Because I'm looking for an excuse to see you again."

"Oh." My mouth goes dry.

"So can I get a private lesson?"

"It'll cost you."

"How much?"

"Lessons are very expensive."

"What time do you get out of work?"

I swallow. "Eight."

"Meet you there?"

"Okay."

"Bye, Harper."

"Bye, Penn."

He hangs up.

My heart is beating so fast, it feels like it's going to burst out of my chest. How can a guy I've just met have this kind of effect on me?

Penn

I wasn't planning on seeing her again. I wasn't even planning on *calling* her.

But after I left school and drove around for a while, I went home, and Braden was being all hyper, and my mom made this huge lunch and everyone was pretending like they weren't bothered by the fact that my dad had taken off again and I was home in the middle of the day.

It was such bullshit, the way the two of them sat there, eating their dumb fried chicken (which wasn't even real fried chicken; it was stupid Shake 'n Bake) and acting like everything was fucking A-OK. Even Braden was pretending like everything was fine, obviously forgetting that he'd called me all panicked just a few hours before. No one even asked me why I was home from school early.

And then for some reason Harper popped into my head. So I looked her up on Facebook, and before I even knew what I was doing, I called her at work.

When I walk into the dance studio at eight, there's a young couple in the front dance room, seemingly in the middle of a lesson.

"No, Jeremy!" the girl screeches. "You need to lead me. I'm the woman! You lead me. Not the other way around."

"I'm trying," Jeremy says. "But it's hard when you keep stepping on my feet."

"This is awful," the girl says. "We've been here for five hours, and it's just not working! Who has a five-hour dance lesson? It's insane! I'm canceling the whole first dance. In fact, maybe I'll just cancel the whole wedding!" She marches over to a little table against the far wall and pulls her cell phone out of her purse. "I'm calling my mom!" she yells. "I'm calling her right now and telling her this dumb wedding is off."

She looks at Jeremy, daring him to stop her. But he just crosses his arms over his chest. "Fine with me." He shrugs. "I wanted to elope anyway."

This infuriates her. She throws her phone down onto the ground, and it smashes into a million pieces.

"Wow," I say, shaking my head. "I didn't know dancing was so dramatic."

The tall woman who's with them, I guess their teacher, turns around and glares at me. She's older, like my mom's age. Her hair is pulled back into a severe bun, and her eyes bore down at me.

"Can I help you?" she asks.

"Yeah, I'm here to see Harper."

"Harper?" She looks surprised.

"Yeah. Harper Fairbanks. She works here, right?"

"Yes, she does." She looks me over. "Are you a friend of hers?"

Huh. I'm not sure how to answer that. "Is she here?" I ask, intentionally avoiding the question while sort of half nodding my head in what might be considered an answer.

Jeremy walks over and picks up his fiancée's ruined phone. I look at him, barely able to contain my disgust. How can he let her treat him that way? "Have some balls, man," I mutter, before I can stop myself.

He turns around, and for a second I think maybe he wants to deck me. But instead he just shakes his head and gives me one of those *What can you do?* kind of looks. Talk about being whipped. Not that I should have expected anything else. The dude's wearing a lime-green shirt.

"Look, is Harper here or not?" I say to the teacher. "Because she told me to meet her here and—"

A door against the side wall opens, and Harper comes walking out.

"Oh," she says when she sees me. "You're here."

"I'm here," I say, looking her up and down. She's wearing the same outfit she had on in school, but she's taken off the white shirt, leaving her in only a tank top and a pair of jeans. I let my eyes wander up her body. Damn. Until just now, I'd never realized how curvy she is. I realize I'm about to have her, alone, in my truck. And then I wonder why I didn't take advantage of that fact earlier. "Ready for my private lesson." I give her a suggestive smile.

"Harper," the woman teacher says, all stern. "Who is this young man?"

Right. I guess I shouldn't have been so glib in front of her boss. But who really cares? It's not like Harper can get fired because I was being a little flirty with her.

"Oh." Harper still looks startled, the way you do when different parts of your life are colliding and you don't really know what to do about it. "This is Penn. Penn, this is my mom."

"I don't think my mom liked you," Harper says as I lead her to my truck.

"You think?" I open the door for her, and I can tell she's impressed. It's not that I like being chivalrous. It's just that I've learned that if you *are* chivalrous, you have a better chance of getting what you want. I know that sounds horrible, and it is. But old habits die hard.

"What did you say to her before I came out?" she asks when I get into the car.

"Nothing." I turn the key in the ignition, and my truck roars to life.

She looks at me skeptically.

"I didn't say anything to her." God, everyone's always so

suspicious of me. "But I said something *around* her that might have gotten her a little annoyed."

"Like what?"

"I told that guy in there that he should grow some balls."

I expect her to turn up her nose and look at me in disgust, because I'm pretty sure a girl who's afraid of the school nurse won't appreciate me using the word "balls" in front of her mom. But instead she just starts laughing. "He *should* grow some balls. You know that's their seventh lesson, and they still don't know the steps."

I shrug. "Is that bad?"

"It's really bad." She shakes her head. "But still. Now my mom's gonna hate you."

I shrug. "No offense, but I don't really give a fuck what your mom thinks about me. Parents don't usually like me."

"Why not?"

"Really?" I raise my eyebrows.

"No." She shakes her head and grins. "It was rhetorical."

"Good." I like the fact that she doesn't care that I'm not trying to make a good impression on her mom. The last thing I want her to think is that this is a date or something. Because it's not. Is it? I can't figure out why I'm here exactly, why I've come back to see her, why I looked her up on Facebook and made a whole effort to try to find out where she was. It's very strange. "So," I say, "you told me you were going to give me a private lesson, but apparently that was a lie."

"I told you I wasn't a teacher."

"Yeah, but aren't you a dancer?"

"I'm a choreographer. I'm good at coming up with steps for people who already have some dance knowledge. I'm not very good at teaching beginners."

I glance at her. "Don't worry," I say. "I'm good at teaching beginners." The words are out of my mouth before I can stop them.

Harper shifts again, then pulls at the sleeves of the shirt she's put back on until they almost cover her wrists. As she moves, her tank top slides down a little in front, exposing some of her cleavage. I avert my eyes.

"Come on," I say, shaking my head and pushing away the less-than-PG thoughts I'm having. "If you can't teach me, then I'll teach you."

Harper

This is weird. I've never really been this close to a boy before. Well, that's not entirely true. I mean, obviously I've been close to guys that I've danced with, and one time I was in a school play with a boy and I had to hold his hand because we were playing frolicking villagers or something.

But this is different. This is me being close to a boy who (a) is insanely hot, (b) left a note on my desk that may or may not mean he's interested in me, and (c) is flirting with me nonstop.

So it's a totally different story.

And okay, here's where things get completely embarrassing. I've never been kissed. Never had a boyfriend, never even played spin the bottle. On the rare occasions when I'd be at a party where some make-out game was being played,

I'd give some excuse about why I couldn't participate.

One time in seventh grade I even made up a fake boyfriend who went to a different school so I could get out of playing. I'm pretty sure no one believed me, but luckily no one called me out on it. Probably because they were all too excited about the fact that they were about to be kissing.

The truth is, I was afraid no one would *want* to kiss me. I was scared the bottle would land on me and whoever had spun it would make a grossed-out face and then refuse.

And even though the kissing stuff excited me, eventually spin the bottle morphed into ninety seconds in heaven, where you'd have to pair off and go into someone's, like, bathroom or rec room (because closets weren't readily available in anyone's basement, which is where these kinds of games were usually played) and do God knows what for a minute and a half. And that terrified me.

So you can see why I might be a little on edge, especially with all that talk about teaching beginners. Does Penn think I'm inexperienced? Is it that obvious?

We stay quiet as he drives, but it's different than it was earlier. Before, I was nervous that Penn might be psycho. Now I'm just nervous.

Finally Penn pulls up in front of the Westville Sports Complex. It's a huge building with one of those white dome ceilings that look like a bubble.

I just stare. "What are we doing here?"

"I told you," he says. "I'm going to teach you."

He hops out of the car and then comes around and opens

the door for me. I like that he's being sweet, even though I'm trying not to like it. It probably doesn't mean anything. It doesn't mean that he likes me.

He probably does things like that for everyone, just to be nice. I need to be careful about reading too much into things. It's just that this thing with Penn is making my head spin. Yesterday I didn't even know him, and now in the span of less than twelve hours, we've hung out twice. If you can call what we did earlier hanging out. Not to mention that he stalked my Facebook page. Why was he stalking my Facebook page? That has to mean he likes me a little, right?

He starts walking toward the door, and I run to catch up with him. The air is hot and muggy, and I can tell my hair is about to turn into a poufy mess. I tug it back into a ponytail.

"Is this . . . I mean, we're not going to be running or anything, are we?" I'm in okay shape because of all the dancing I do, but I'm a horrible runner. I'm not fast at all. When we run the mile at school, I'm always one of the last ones to finish.

Penn holds the door open, and I step inside and am immediately greeted by the cold air of the air-conditioned building. "Why?" he asks, giving me a sexy little grin. "You planning on trying to run away from me?"

"No." I shake my head. "I just want to know what kind of footwear I'm going to need." I gesture down to my feet, which are encased in my brown strappy sandals. Thank God I gave myself a pedicure last night. My toenails are painted a soft pink color, perfect for early summer.

"Oh." Penn seems dismayed. "Yeah, we're definitely going to have to do something about those."

"What?" I ask. But he's already moving through the doors. "What am I going to have to wear?" I have a thing with shoes. I don't like wearing shoes that other people have worn. Like if I go bowling or something, I get totally freaked out. That's how you end up with a foot fungus.

"Relax," Penn says. "You can wear those if you really want to."

"I *am* relaxed."

"Really?" He shakes his head like I'm a hopeless case.

Once we're inside, I realize that we're in the part of the sports complex that's a ballpark. Like, an indoor ballpark. There's a big baseball diamond in the middle, and there are guys on the field, swinging bats, playing catch, and stretching. Bleachers line the walls, and there's even tall stadium lights shining down onto the field.

"Baseball?" I ask. "I don't know how to play baseball. Is that what you're going to teach me? Because I'm not that coordinated. I mean, I am with some stuff, obviously, since I'm a choreographer. But with hand-eye coordination, you know, I'm not that good." I realize that I'm babbling, and I twist my hands and try to calm down.

Penn closes his eyes, like it pains him that I'm asking questions. "No, Harper," he says. "I'm not going to teach you how to play baseball. Playing baseball is not something I can teach you in just a couple of hours. But I can try to teach you how to hit."

Hit? Like bat baseballs? What is he talking about? I just told him I have horrible hand-eye coordination.

Penn steps up to the front desk before I can figure out how I'm going to get out of this whole thing. The guy who's working the desk is wearing a red polo shirt. He looks like an athlete—tall, tan skin, a little older than us, probably in college.

"Hey, Ian," Penn says as he pulls out his wallet. "You home for break?"

"Yup." Ian sighs. "Only working here a couple of days though. Then I'm headed down to Florida for a tournament." He mimes pitching a ball. "It never stops, you know?"

"I hear ya." But Penn's voice doesn't sound all that friendly.

"I heard you've been trying to get in with Dr. Marzetti," Ian says.

"I haven't really decided yet," Penn says. He's holding his debit card, and he taps it against the counter impatiently.

"Really?" Ian persists. "Because that's what I heard from Coach."

"Yeah, well, like I said, I haven't decided yet."

Wow. This whole thing is getting kind of intense. And the guy behind the counter must realize it, because he turns his attention to me. He slides his eyes up me the way that boys do when they're checking you out. He grins at Penn, and I can't tell exactly what his grin means. It's very . . . sort of smarmy. Like maybe he thinks that Penn is going to have sex with me? Or it could be one of those grins, like, *Oh, Penn strikes again.* I wonder how many other girls Penn has brought here, and I decide it's probably a lot.

I've seen him in the halls at school, girls trailing after him. Of course, most of the times I can remember that happening were when Penn was still on the baseball team.

"You ready?" Penn asks me.

"Oh. Yeah."

I follow him across the field to the back of the building and through some double doors marked BATTING CAGES. Back here there's no one around and everything's quiet.

"Wow," I say. "How come no one's practicing?"

"Because none of them think they need to," Penn says. He walks over to one of the racks against the wall and picks up a helmet. "Here," he says, handing it to me.

I look at it. "What's this for?"

"So you don't get hit in the head."

"Yeah, I know what a helmet is."

He sighs. "Then why'd you ask?"

"I just meant why'd you give me this one?"

He shrugs. "It's pink."

"And you just assumed that because I'm a girl I like pink?"

"Well, yeah." He has the decency to look sheepish.

"This helmet is for a child." It's true. The pink helmet he gave me is for a little girl. Or a little boy. I'm not going to be all sexist the way Penn was and just *assume* that only a little girl could use it. Boys can like pink too. My little cousin Jeremiah likes to wear pink tutus during preschool dress-up time. At least he did until his parents freaked out and pulled him out of that school because they thought it was too progressive.

"Oh." Penn takes the helmet from me. "Well, what about

this one?" He picks up a black one and puts it on my head. It slides down over my eyes.

I push it back up. He laughs and shakes his head. "It's too big for you."

"No, it's not." I strike a pose and puff out my bottom lip. "It makes me look like a badass."

Penn shakes his head, then walks over to one of the cages.

I become painfully aware that now that I'm wearing a helmet, he's probably going to expect me to actually hit.

I follow him over to the batting cage, and he pulls a bat out from a bag that's sitting against the wall.

I pick one up and try to pretend I know what I'm doing. I swing it around in circles.

"What are you doing?" Penn asks.

"Just, you know, warming up." I toss it around a little more, hoping I look casual and natural.

"You're holding that baseball bat like a golf club."

"No, I'm not!" I quickly pick the bat up and rest it against my shoulder.

"Now you're holding it like a purse." He shakes his head. He steps behind me and puts his arms around my shoulders, showing me how to hold the bat. He smells like soap and vanilla and Axe body spray.

He swings my arms for me and little jolts of electricity fly through my body.

"Now, keep your eye on the ball," he says.

A ball comes flying out of one of the machines, and I jump

back and scream. "Ahhh!" I drop the bat, and Penn laughs.

"What the hell?" I say. "I wasn't expecting that!"

"It's on a timer," he says. "Sorry. I should have warned you."

"Wow," I say. "What if I'd been hit? What if I'd *died*?"

"You weren't going to get hit," Penn says. He comes over and stands in front of me. "I would never have let you get hit."

He's staring at me with intensity, and I know he's telling me the truth. I don't know why, but I have the feeling that he would never put me in harm's way.

"Fine, whatever, " I say, mostly because I can't handle the way he's looking at me. "Can I try it again?"

"Course."

He puts his arms back around me. I'm finding it hard to concentrate when he's this close. Another ball comes flying, and I feel his arms tighten, and then he's swinging, and we make contact with the ball. It goes flying to the back of the cage.

"And that," he says triumphantly, "is how you do it."

We hit a few more balls, but his arms against mine are giving me goose bumps and making me feel dizzy. After a few minutes I step back.

"Had enough?" He grins.

"Kind of," I say. "My arms are getting sore."

He hits a few balls by himself, and I watch as his biceps flex. I try not to stare, but he's good. Like, really good. The balls go flying all the way over the fence that's against the back wall, and I can tell he was taking it easy on me. He's strong.

I shiver, because it's actually very sexy.

"So," I say when the machine finally stops and Penn takes a break. "Why'd you stop playing?"

"Because the machine ran out of balls."

"No, I mean . . . like, in general. How come you're not on the team anymore?"

Penn shrugs. "Got hurt."

"And you're still hurt?"

"No. Well, I mean, I'm not in pain anymore."

"Then why aren't you still playing ball?"

He swings the bat and then tosses it onto the ground. "You ask a lot of questions."

"You don't ask enough."

He grins and then crouches down and slides the bat back into the bag. "Yeah? And what am I supposed to ask you?"

"I don't know. Isn't there anything you want to know about me?"

He shrugs. "You told me all that fascinating stuff about yourself earlier, remember? And I already know you're cool, you're smart, and that you have medical anxiety."

"I don't have medical anxiety!" I notice that he didn't call me cute, and I wonder if I should be offended. Do I want him to think I'm cute? I think again about how it felt when he had his arms around me a moment ago, and my pulse starts to race.

"Then why are you running from the nurse?"

"I'm not running from the nurse!" I think about it. "I'm hiding from her."

He shrugs, then zips up the bag of bats and stands back up. "Whatever. Same difference."

"Not really," I say. "If I was running from her, I would have literally been running."

"I meant running more in the metaphorical sense."

"I know that."

He takes off his helmet and shakes out his hair. His hair is a little bit shaggy, like he needs a haircut. He doesn't look messy or anything, though. It just looks sexy. I swallow as he throws his helmet down onto the ground. A heat is moving through my body, starting in my toes and sliding up through my torso. I wonder what we're going to do now. Is he going to take me home?

Before I can figure out if I want him to, the door to the batting cages opens, and two guys come strolling in. They're both wearing navy-blue T-shirts and white track pants, the kind that snap up the side. They're talking and laughing in that way guys do, the way that makes it clear they're talking about something unsavory, like a girl they had sex with or how drunk they were the other night.

"I'm telling you," one of them says, "it's true."

"I don't doubt it," the other guy says. "That's so hilarious." He draws out the word, making it sound like hi-*lar*-ious.

They move closer, and I recognize the taller one. It's Jackson Burr. He's in our class at school. I've never had much contact with him, though. He's the type of guy I've always been afraid of—good-looking and unpredictable.

His gaze lands on Penn. "Well, well, well," he drawls, "if it isn't Mr. Mattingly himself. To what do we owe the honor?"

Penn shrugs, like the question is no big deal, but his shoulders tense up and his jaw sets into a straight line. "Just hitting."

"Oh, yeah?" Jackson smiles and then looks at me, his eyes moving up my body, like maybe Penn was talking about hitting something else. "Who's your friend?" I try not to feel insulted. Jackson Burr and I have been in a few of the same classes every year since we were freshman. You'd think he'd at least know my name.

Penn shrugs. "No one."

Jackson must agree with him, because he turns his gaze away from me, like I'm dismissed. Wow. Talk about every single boy cliché happening in, like, the space of four minutes. Two guys talking like they think they're the shit? Check. A guy writing me off because I don't have blond hair and big boobs? Check.

I can't believe Penn insisted I come here with him, and now he's, like, pretending it means nothing.

"I have a name," I say. I reach my hand out to Jackson. He looks back at me, surprised, almost like he's startled that I'm there, even though a second ago he was undressing me with his eyes. "I'm Harper."

"Harper," Jackson says, like he's never heard the name before. He reaches out and takes my hand. His hand is rough and kind of cold. "I'm Jackson."

I think about telling him that I already know his name, that he's been in a bunch of my classes, but then I figure, what's the point? All it will do is give him a big head, that a girl he's never noticed before knows who he is. So all I say is, "Nice to meet you."

"Nice to meet you, too."

Penn's just standing there, still all tense.

Jackson's friend is over in the corner, looking through a bag of bats, almost like he's bored with this whole interaction.

"So," I say. "Um, you guys were on the baseball team together?"

"Oh, me and Penn go way back," Jackson says. "We're old friends. Aren't we, Penn?"

"Sure," Penn says. But he's not smiling. He turns to me. "We should get going."

"You don't have to leave on account of me," Jackson says. "Stick around. We can hit together, like old times."

I'm about to say I don't mind, that if they want to hit together, I'll just hang out and watch them practice, but I can tell Penn doesn't want to. It's weird. His whole vibe has changed. Before he was light and flirty, and now there's a darkness permeating through him.

"No." Penn shakes his head. "Come on, Harper."

Jackson smiles again. "Okay," he says. "Maybe another time." Then he turns and looks at me. "I hope to see you around again, Harper. Don't be a stranger, okay?"

I have no idea what he's talking about, and then I get it. He's trying to flirt with me because he wants to annoy Penn. I mean, think about it—when Jackson looked at me before, he pretty much wanted nothing to do with me. And now all of a sudden he's going out of his way to talk to me? It's obviously just to get under Penn's skin. Is it working? Is it wrong that I hope it is?

I turn around to look at Penn, to see if he's maybe getting all jealous over Jackson talking to me.

But I can't see his face.

He's already walking out of the batting cages, leaving me no choice but to run after him.

Penn

I hate Jackson Burr. He's the biggest asshole I've ever met, and what just happened is a perfect example of why. That dude doesn't give a shit about me or what I'm doing, and the only reason he even asks me that stuff is because he's hoping I'm going to tell him bad news. He *wants* me to tell him bad news. He gets off on it.

I'm halfway out the front door of the athletic complex before I realize Harper is following me. Jesus. I almost forgot she was with me.

"Hey!" she yells. She's struggling to walk across the parking lot in her strappy sandals. It must have rained while we were inside, because the sky is overcast and the pavement is dark and slick. Harper's dodging little puddles as she races to catch up. "Hold on a second, would you?"

I slow down reluctantly. My body is filled with energy, and I don't want to stop moving. "Sorry," I say.

"What the hell was that about?" She takes a few more steps toward me, and then takes a big jump over a wider puddle, but she doesn't quite clear it. Her foot splashes rainwater onto her shin.

"Shit," she swears. She looks down at her soaked sandal, perplexed, like she can't believe what's happened. I try not to laugh.

I'm at my truck now, so I reach into the backseat, pull out a towel, and take it back to her. Harper looks at it doubtfully.

I roll my eyes. "It's fine," I say. "It's not that dirty."

"Not *that* dirty?"

"Yeah." I shrug. "I probably used it, like, once." That towel's been in my truck for God knows how long, so I really can't say for sure if I've used it once or a hundred times. But seriously, what does she think is going to happen? It's just a towel.

"What if I get flesh-eating bacteria?" she asks.

"You're kidding, right?"

"Sort of."

"My towel doesn't have flesh-eating bacteria."

"I'm not saying *you* have flesh-eating bacteria. I'm just saying that—"

"Good. Because I don't. And therefore, neither does my towel."

"Well, your towel technically could even if you don't. Your towel could have come into contact with flesh-eating bacteria on its own. Or some other kind of bacteria. And it could have infiltrated the—"

Oh, Jesus Christ. I lean down and start drying off her foot with the towel.

"Hey!" she yells. "What do you think you're doing." She tries to kick the towel off, and her sandal goes flying through the air and lands in another puddle.

"Great," I say, shaking my head sadly. "Now see what you've done?"

"What *I've* done?" She's standing on one foot and she's having trouble keeping her balance, so she puts her arms out to keep from falling over. I walk over and pick up her shoe.

"Yeah," I say. "If you'd just let me clean you off without freaking out, you wouldn't have lost your shoe."

She glares at me and then takes a few hops. And that's when she loses her balance and her bare foot steps right into a puddle.

"Oh God," I say, mostly because I can't resist. "Now you're definitely going to get flesh-eating bacteria. It probably lives in that stagnant water."

"No, it doesn't!" She pulls her foot out of the water like it's radioactive, and starts to sort of hobble toward the car.

"Oh, no way," I say, rushing to catch up with her. "You are not getting into my car with a dirty foot."

"You've got to be kidding," she says. "With all those straw wrappers you have on the floor? Now you're worried about a little bit of dirt?"

I'm insulted that she's insinuating I'm a slob. Yeah, maybe there are a few random straw wrappers on the floor of my car. But a few straw wrappers do not a slob make.

"Relax," Harper says. "I'm not going to mess up your precious car."

She's still hopping on one leg, a little faster now, and I have a flash of her slipping and falling and cracking her head on the pavement. I run to catch up with her.

"Let me help you," I say, putting my arm around her waist.

She tries to push me away. "I'm okay."

"Please," I say, and tighten my grip. "The last time you tried to push me away, your shoe ended up in a puddle."

"Good point," she grumbles. Her one sandaled foot slips on the pavement and she leans into me to keep from falling. As she does, her hair brushes against my cheek, and I'm surprised at how soft it is. She smells like flowers and coconut.

I lead her over to my car and open the door for her, then sit her down and finish wiping her foot off with the towel. Then I clean off her wet shoe and hand it back to her, before tossing the towel into the backseat.

"Thanks," she says as she slips her sandal back on. She sounds shy, and her hair is falling over her face, making her look pretty adorable.

"You're welcome."

She scrunches up her lips and pushes them over to the side, like she's thinking about something. The light is shining through the windshield, illuminating her face, and I think that maybe I'm going to have to kiss her. Which is weird. Because she's way too nice for me to kiss.

Then why did you bring her here with you? Why were you thinking about her all day?

"So what's the deal with you and Jackson?" she asks. She bends her legs and sort of pulls them against her chest, folding herself into my car sideways.

I'm still thinking about what it would be like to kiss her, so I move away and lean against the car, making it harder for me to see her.

"What do you mean?"

"I mean, why was there all that tension?"

"There wasn't tension."

"Fine." She shrugs. "You don't have to tell me if you don't want to."

"I don't not want to tell you. It's just that there's nothing to tell."

She sighs. "You're secretive, I get it. Obviously something very painful happened and you don't want to get into it. It's not a big deal, Penn. I'm not, like, *offended* or anything."

I glance down at her, wondering if she's joking. "You've got to be kidding me."

"No."

I shake my head. "Look, Jackson and I used to be friends. And now we're not anymore. There's nothing to tell." There's a lot more to tell. But I'm not going to talk about it with

Harper. I don't talk about it with anyone. Not Jackson. Not even myself. And so there's no way I'm going to talk about it with some girl I just met. Even if she is hot and adorable all at once.

I can feel my mood darkening.

"Okay," Harper says. I expect her to press me on things, but she doesn't say anything else.

"Look," I say. "I should probably take you home."

The last thing I want to do is take her home. I want to keep her with me. And besides, *I* don't want to go home. There's nothing there for me, except Braden zoned out in front of the television, and my mom probably bustling around the kitchen, baking or doing something equally ridiculous, given the fact that my dad is gone again.

"Yeah," Harper says. "I should get back. My mom's probably freaking out about where I am."

But she doesn't move, and neither do I.

The door to the sports arena opens, and Jackson comes walking out. He heads over to his car and pulls some batting gloves out of the trunk, then disappears back inside.

Me and Harper just watch him, silently.

"So," I say after a moment, "you want to go get something to eat?"

Harper

Is this a date? I can't tell. I think it might be a date. We went to the batting cages and now we're going to get something to eat. So we must be on a date. I mean, think about it. If someone said to you, "Hey, you wanna go to the batting cages and then maybe go out and get something to eat?" you'd think that was a date. Wouldn't you?

And yeah, Penn didn't exactly call me up and ask me if I wanted to do that stuff, it kind of just happened. But still.

"Where are we going to eat?" I ask. I haven't had anything since lunch, but I don't feel hungry. In fact, my stomach is filled with butterflies, and they're swarming around and making me feel jittery. I'm thinking about how his hands brushed against my skin, and it's making me all flushed.

Penn looks at me. "I don't like restaurants."

"Oh." I'm not really sure what to say to that. How come he asked me out to eat if he doesn't like restaurants? I glance at him suspiciously. He better not think this is going to be one of those things where he pretends he's taking me out to eat and then he takes me somewhere else and tries to get me to make out with him. I don't make out with people on first dates. Not that I've had that many first dates. Or that many make-out sessions.

He doesn't say anything, but he's pulled the car out onto the main road, and he's heading in the opposite direction from my house and the dance studio.

"So then where are we going?" I ask.

He shrugs. "It stopped raining. We can eat at the park."

"You mean like a picnic?" Why does he want to have a picnic in the dark? I want to ask him, but I'm afraid that if I do, he'll take back the invitation.

He glances at me. "No, not a picnic, Harper. Just eating outside."

I frown. "Eating outside sounds like a picnic."

"I don't do picnics."

"Eating outside at a park is a picnic." I shrug. "Just admit you like picnics, Penn. It's nothing to be embarrassed about."

"I'm not *embarrassed* about anything."

"Okay."

"But it's not a picnic."

I pull out my phone and start to google the definition of

"picnic." "Picnic," I recite, "an outing or occasion that involves taking packed food outdoors for a meal."

He gapes at me. "Did you just google that?"

"That's what Google's for."

"Google's not for—" He cuts himself off and shakes his head, like he can't believe we're having this conversation. "Whatever. We're not packing any food. We're just buying it, so it's not a picnic."

He pulls into a Whole Foods and cuts the engine. "You stay here," he instructs.

"How come?"

"Because I can shop faster by myself." He looks at me. "No offense, but girls take way too long in the store. And it's already dark."

"First of all, that's extremely sexist. And second of all, I don't take a long time in the store." It's a lie. I take a very long time in the store. But how could Penn possibly know this?

He raises his eyebrows, like he's considering it. Then, a second later, he shakes his head. "You stay here." And then he's out of the car and on his way into the store.

As soon as he's gone, I pull out my phone and call Anna.

She picks up on the first ring.

"What's wrong?" she asks immediately.

"Nothing," I say. "Why would something be wrong?"

"Because you never call me. You always text."

"Oh. Well, I have limited time." I flip the passenger-side visor down. But there's no mirror on the other side. What?

81

Why? How can a car not have a mirror on the visor? How am I supposed to make sure I don't have dirty puddle water splashed on my face or in my hair or something?

"What do you mean you have limited time? Are you at work? I thought your mom got over that whole not-using-your-phone-during-work-hours thing?"

"She did." I reach over to Penn's side of the car and flip down his visor. There's a mirror on that one. Which is ironic, since I'm the one who needs the mirror, and Penn doesn't seem like the kind of guy who spends any time whatsoever checking himself out. Which kind of doesn't make sense, since he's so good-looking. I always figured anyone that hot would enjoy looking at himself all the time. Does Penn not know how cute he is? I have another flash of him walking down the hall at school, always with a different girl. So he must.

"Hello?" Anna calls. "What are you doing? What's all the commotion?"

"I'm in Penn Mattingly's car." I whisper it. I don't know why. Penn is in the store, and there's no one in the parking lot. And even if there were, who cares if someone overhears?

"You're where?" Anna yells, like she's trying to make up for the fact that I'm whispering. "I can't hear a word you're saying. Speak up."

"I'm in Penn Mattingly's car," I say, louder this time. The words sound foreign and kind of exciting. I'm in a boy's car. A boy I hardly know. It sounds almost dangerous.

"Penn Mattingly's car!" Anna sounds excited.

"Shh!" I'm trying to grab at the visor and angle it so I can see my reflection. But I'm having trouble, so I have to sling one foot over the gearshift. I pull the mirror toward me, and am grateful to see that I don't have anything on my face. But my eye makeup is a little smudged, and so I reach up and wipe it away.

"Why do I have to shhh?" Anna asks defensively. Then I hear her say to someone in the background, "Harper's on a date with Penn Mattingly!" She's probably talking to Nico. Nico is Anna's best friend besides me. Well, if you can count a boy who you're secretly in love with as your second best friend, which Anna thinks you can.

"It's not a date." Trying to fix my makeup with my finger isn't working. In fact, I'm just making it worse. I go to reach for my purse, but somehow my legs sort of splay apart, and I end up knocking my purse over onto the passenger-side floor. "Shit!"

"What happened?" Anna asks.

"I knocked my purse over."

"In his car? How'd you knock your purse over in his car?" Suddenly she's suspicious, like she thinks I'm up to no good.

"I was trying to look at myself in the mirror."

"She was trying to look at herself in the mirror," Anna reports to Nico.

"Don't tell him that!" I say. I'm not sure why, but I don't want Nico to know what's going on. This is one of those times when the fact that he's male definitely gets in the way of me being able to give him information. Plus, I've never been as close to Nico as Anna is. And I don't think he should get secrets about me just because I'm telling them to Anna.

"Why not? It's just Nico."

"Because I don't want him knowing everything."

"It's not like you and Penn are hooking up. Are you? Have you? Did you kiss him? Did he kiss you?"

"No!" I say. "It's not . . . I mean, it's not a date." But suddenly I'm thinking about kissing him. He looks like he'd be a good kisser. Probably strong, but not too strong, with just the right amount of—

The driver-side door opens, and I scream in surprise, then immediately fall over into the passenger seat.

Penn is standing there. He looks down at me, my legs sprawled between the seats. He shakes his head. "Wow," he says. "I leave you alone for one minute . . ."

"Um, I gotta go," I say to Anna, scrambling back over to my side of the car.

"What?" she screeches. "Harper, you can't just—"

I hang up. I'm kind of humiliated. "Can I get in now?" Penn asks. He seems amused.

"Yes," I say haughtily. "Of course you can get in." I put my nose up in the air and roll my eyes, like he's being ridiculous. Which he kind of is. This is his car. Of course he can get into his own car. He doesn't have to ask my permission.

"Okay, good," he says. He flings the Whole Foods bags into the backseat. "Just didn't know if you wanted to be alone."

My face is burning. God, he must think I'm a complete and total head case. "I'm fine." I catch a glimpse of myself in the side mirror, and my face is still streaked with eyeliner. I reach up and rub it off. There's no way I can fix it with Penn here, watching, so I'll have to just deal with having raccoon eyes for now.

"Okay." He shrugs and puts the car into drive.

He takes me to Schoner Park and parks near the swings, right on the lawn. It's after nine o'clock now, and so the place is deserted.

He pulls the bags of food out from the back of his car and sets them down on the hood of his truck.

"You're going to be impressed," he says, sounding proud of himself.

"Really? Why?"

"Well," he says, "you probably have this impression of me. You know, that I'm just some jock ballplayer who knows nothing about anything else."

"I don't really have any impression of you, except for that maybe you're a stalker."

"A stalker?"

"Yeah, like how you showed up at my work and stalked me."

He shakes his head. "I don't stalk."

"Whatever."

We hoist ourselves onto the hood of the truck, and Penn reaches into the bags and starts laying out the food he bought.

I have to say that he was right—it is impressive. Stone-ground wheat pepper crackers, cut up strawberries and honeydew, goat cheese, fig and walnut spread, and two tiny plastic containers filled with bow tie pasta salad.

He hands me a plastic fork, and as he does, his hand brushes against mine.

"Thanks." Goose bumps fly up my skin.

"You're welcome." All trace of the teasing he was doing before is gone, and now he just sounds . . . I don't know, sort of serious and sort of sexy at the same time.

I grab the crackers and start to open the box. Inside there are two sleeves, and my fingers fumble around the plastic. When I finally get them open, I realize there's nowhere to put them, so I pull a few out and lay them down on the cracker box.

"So," I say. The air feels heavy all of a sudden. Yes, it's because it rained, and because it's humid, but it's also because things have shifted. It's subtle, but it's there. Before when I was with Penn, there was a lot of activity around us—we were at the dance studio, or the batting cages, or something, and now . . . now we're just here, sitting on his car with nothing to do but . . . talk.

"So," he replies.

I take a cracker and dip it into the goat cheese spread. It's delicious.

"Is this where you used to play baseball?" I ask, gazing out onto the field.

I'm not sure if it's my imagination or not, but I feel like he stiffens beside me. "No," he says. He takes a swig of water. "Well, not recently. I played here when I was a kid."

"Oh. And you . . . I mean, are you going to play in college?" I know he hurt his shoulder. I know he doesn't play anymore. I want to know if he's going to get better, but I'm not sure exactly how to ask him that.

He shrugs, then just gazes out onto the baseball field. Then, suddenly, he jumps off the hood of the car until he's standing in front of me. He leans in close to me and gives me a devilish smile.

"Hi," he says, and that's when I know he's going to kiss me.

I hardly even know him, and he's going to kiss me. Which is crazy. But what's even crazier is that I want him to kiss me. I want to kiss him so bad, I can hardly take it.

He reaches up and pushes a piece of hair back from my forehead, and his eyes are gazing right into mine, and it's so perfect and romantic and passionate that I swear it feels like I'm in a movie.

"Hi," I breathe.

He moves his face closer to mine, and then he kisses me. His lips are cool, but his mouth is warm and his kiss is soft. It takes us less than a second to find a rhythm. He wraps his arms around my waist and pulls me against him.

A breeze ruffles the trees and sends a shiver up my spine, and I'm not sure if it's because the air has gotten colder or because of the kiss. He pulls back for a minute, and then his lips are back on mine, teasing me. He's kissing me the exact way I thought he would—strong and firm and perfect. His face is smooth, but there's a little bit of stubble rubbing against my chin, and I lose all track of time as his lips move against mine. My heart is beating fast, and my skin is flushed. My lips are getting swollen from the kissing, and my hair is getting tangled in his fingers.

When he finally pulls away, he trails his fingers up my arms, sending tingles flying through my body.

"Well," he says. "I guess that happened."

"Yeah," I whisper. "I guess it did."

Penn

I shouldn't have kissed her. I knew that as soon as I did it. It's just that she'd been sitting there looking so adorable, trying to open that damn package of crackers. How could opening a package of crackers look cute? It made no sense.

But it was more than that. Not only is she cute, but let's face it, she is also hot. And I was stupid for not noticing it earlier. Although I guess I must have noticed it a little bit—I did put that note on her desk, after all. But that note was a throwaway, something I did on the spur of the moment. It's not like I wanted anything to come of it. If I want a girl, I don't waste time with cute little notes. That's what guys who have no game do. That's what guys who want romance do.

And I'm not that guy.

But now I've gone and kissed Harper, and to make it even worse, I did it on the hood of my car after a rainstorm, at a park while we were having a picnic. What the *hell* was I thinking?

After we kiss, I expect things to be awkward, like it usually is after you kiss a girl for the first time. But it's not.

We sit. We eat.

Harper asks me questions about my family (which I dodge), about baseball (which I dodge), about school (fine, whatever), and about how I got to be so good at picking out picnic food (completely safe, because I bullshit it and tell her that I'm into watching the Food Network. Which is true, but only because it's one of the only channels that doesn't have infomercials on late at night, and so I watch it when I can't fall asleep.)

I'm having a nice time. Like, a really nice time. The nicest time I can ever remember having with a girl. But as I'm driving her home, I can feel my mood starting to darken.

Yes, I had a nice time with Harper, but that doesn't erase the million things that happened today that could have set me off. Like seeing Jackson, or the fact that I'm on my way home and I have no idea what I'm going to find there.

"So," Harper says when I pull into her driveway. She fiddles with the strap of her bag. "I guess . . . I mean, I guess I'll see you in school tomorrow." She looks at me, and I can see in her eyes that she wants some reassurance. She wants me to tell her that we'll talk tomorrow, that me kissing her meant something.

But I can't give her that.

So instead I just say, "See you tomorrow, Harper."

I watch her walk into the house, until she's inside safely and has shut the door behind her. I imagine her walking up the stairs, dropping her bag in her room, maybe calling a friend or starting her homework.

It's all so normal.

And that's why Harper and I could never work out.

Because she's normal.

And I'm anything but.

When I get home, Braden's sitting on the couch playing video games, and my mom's in the kitchen baking cupcakes. It's ten o'clock at night, and my dad's car is still gone. He's probably on a bender, although it's impossible to know exactly where. He could be drinking himself to death in a hotel room, or a bar, or at a casino. Sometimes I wonder if he has a completely different family, like those people you see on the news who go missing and then turn out to have secret lives. Maybe my dad goes to visit his other family, and they all get drunk and watch sports before passing out in front of the TV.

"Hey!" my mom says happily when she sees me. She holds out a spoonful of batter, like it's normal to be cooking so late at night. "Here," she says. "Taste this."

"Mom," I say, "that stuff is poison."

She frowns and wrinkles her nose at the bowl. "Penn, if you're talking about salmonella, I got these eggs fresh from—"

"I'm not talking about salmonella, Mom." I grab a bottle of

water from the fridge, uncap it, and down almost all of it in one gulp. "I'm talking about the fact that there's tons of hydrogenated fat in there. Plus the dairy alone is filled with hormones."

My mom smiles and shakes her head, like she's exasperated with me. "My son the college athlete," she says proudly. "Always worried about what he puts into his body. Not all of us have to worry about our performance on the baseball field, you know."

I don't say anything, but my mood darkens even more. We both know I'm not playing baseball right now, that I probably won't ever again, and that I definitely won't be playing for a college.

And with my chances of a baseball scholarship completely dashed, there's really no way I'm even *going* to college. Which means I'll be stuck here, probably working at some shitty job that I hate. But my mom doesn't like talking about that. If you ask her, she'll tell you that of course some college is going to take me. She lives in denial—about my shoulder, about my dad, about pretty much everything.

"Well, have fun," I say. I try to keep the sharpness out of my voice. I don't blame her for my dad taking off, but I do blame her for not talking about it, and for not confronting him about it, and for not leaving him years ago.

I walk into the living room, where Braden's zoned out in front of the TV. I can tell just by looking at him that he's high. His eyes are all red and he's slumped against the back of the couch. A half-eaten bag of chips is sitting in front of him on the coffee table.

"Yo," he says, giving me a half salute. He gestures to the other controller. "You want to play?"

I shrug and pick up the controller, and we sit there for a few minutes, blowing things up on the screen. It's supposed to be mindless. And it is. I'm not thinking about Jackson, or my dad, or baseball.

But what I can't stop thinking about is Harper.

But instead of getting me excited, all it does is make me angry. What the hell was I thinking, taking her on a picnic? I'm not in any shape to be taking girls on picnics, especially not girls like Harper. She's too innocent. She works in a dance studio, for God's sake. She wants to be a choreographer. That sounds so . . . I don't know. Pure.

My mind is racing, and I don't realize I'm gripping the controller so hard, until I look down and see the indent the plastic is creating on my hand.

"I need to get out of here," I say, tossing the controller onto the couch.

"Aww, come on," Braden says, shooting at my guys on the screen. "I'm just about to kill you."

I ignore him.

I walk through the kitchen and out the door, and as I do, my mom doesn't even ask me where I'm going. Instead she just waves and says, "See you later, honey!" like it's totally normal for her seventeen-year-old son to be leaving at ten at night.

I drive around for a while, not sure where I'm going.

Until, eventually, I end up at the same place I always end up.

At Sienna's house.

Which is no good.

Not for me.

Not for her.

Not for Harper.

Not for anyone.

Harper

Two weeks. That's how long it's been since Penn kissed me. That's how long it's been since Penn *talked* to me.

Two. Whole. Weeks.

I never realized how long two weeks could be, and I've had a lot of long two weeks. Like the last two weeks of school. Or freshman year, when my mom found a weird lump in her throat and they thought maybe she had thyroid cancer, and by the time she went in for an ultrasound and got the tests results back saying she was fine, it had been two weeks and I was going absolutely crazy.

So it's not like I don't know that fourteen days can be a long time.

The problem, I think, is that this time there's no end in

sight. I knew, with my mom, that we would find something out at some point. And with school ending, I knew the waiting wasn't going to last forever.

But this—I don't know when (or if) it's going to end.

I'm acting like I don't care. I'm acting like I'm not even thinking about it, when in actuality it's *all* I can think about. The way Penn's lips felt on mine, the way his arms encircled my waist, the way the air smelled like rain and early summer, the way he'd somehow known exactly what food to get for our picnic.

He's acting like nothing happened between us, acting like he doesn't even know me, acting like he didn't put a stupid note on my desk saying he liked my sparkle and then stalked me down at work before whisking me off on a picnic, where he kissed me without me even asking him to.

Why? *Why* is he acting this way?

Trying to figure out why a person would do something like that, while simultaneously pretending you don't care, when it's all you can really think about, is completely exhausting.

"I just don't know what song I should do," Anna's saying. "What do you think, Harper?"

"For what?" I ask.

We're sitting outside at McDonald's during our lunch period. Juniors and seniors are allowed to leave during lunch, as long as we stay on the main street near school. How they think they're going to enforce this, I have no idea, since it's not like they can follow every one of us and try to figure out where it is we're spending our lunch period.

"For my Juilliard application!" She throws her hands up and looks over at Nico, who's sitting next to me. "Is she spacey lately, or what?"

"She's definitely spacey lately," Nico says, nodding. It figures he would take her side. This is why I hate when the three of us hang out. "What's going on, Harper?"

"Nothing!" I say.

"I think it has to do with Penn," Anna says. She leans over and studies me, then rests her chin on her hands. The long sleeves of her gauzy black shirt almost skim the pile of ketchup she's set up near her fries.

"It is not about Penn!"

"It's definitely about Penn," Nico says, like he knows something about it.

"Def," Anna agrees. Then they start to do this thing they do sometimes that really annoys me. They talk about me like I'm not there. I know Anna does it because it makes her feel closer to Nico, and I know she doesn't mean anything by it. But still. It's irritating as hell.

"I think they had sex," Nico says.

"No way," Anna says. She picks up a fry and twirls it around in the air, like she's contemplating. "Harper wouldn't have had sex with him. She'd make him wait. But they might have kissed."

"I don't know," Nico says. "Harper might have been too smart for that."

"Too smart?" Anna asks.

"Yeah," Nico replies, then takes a sip of his soda. "She knows Penn is the kiss-'em-and-leave-'em type. So she might have slept with him just to make sure she got what she could, while she could."

"Penn's not like that," I say before I can stop myself. I can't help it. I don't like them saying bad things about him, even though they're obviously true. Penn must be the kiss-'em-and-leave-'em type. I mean, look what he's doing to me.

"Oooh, I think she's sticking up for him," Anna teases.

"She is," Nico says. "She's sticking up for him even though he's a total douche."

"He's not a douche," I say.

"He is," Nico says. "He used to be a total douche when he was on the baseball team, walking around like he was this big man on campus, and then as soon as he got hurt, he dropped all his friends and became angry." He rolls his eyes. "What a baby."

"I don't know. I think it's kind of sexy the way he's always walking around scowling," Anna says. She glances at me out of the corner of her eye. "And I think Harper does too."

She's right. I do like the way Penn is always scowling. Every once in a while, though, I'll catch him smiling, and it makes my heart skip. Not that I look at him all that much. Only when I know I can get away with it, which isn't that often, since he sits behind me in the one class we have together. Which is another added pressure. I'm always worried that he's looking at me in class, so I make sure that I'm sitting up straight, and that my hair is falling perfectly down my back. Which I know is ridiculous, because there's no way he's even looking at me. And the reason I know this is because anytime I've been looking at *him*, he's not looking at me. Not even once.

"Oooh, she's getting red," Anna says, elbowing Nico.

But he's already bored of the conversation, and he's texting on his phone.

"I'm not getting red," I say, even though I can feel my cheeks heating up. I'm annoyed, so I crumple my paper fry container into a little ball and wipe the salty grease off my fingers with a napkin. "I think I'm going to go back to school. I have a paper to work on anyway."

"Oh, come on, Harper," Anna says. "Don't take it so personally. We were just goofing around. Weren't we, Nico?"

She turns to him for help, but she's lost him. He's still texting on his phone, probably with his friends from the basketball team, or one of the girls he's always trying to get with.

"I'm out," he says, standing up and totally ignoring Anna's comment. He turns and looks at me. "We were just teasing you, Harper," he says, his eyes softening. "Sorry if you're upset." He squeezes my shoulder as he passes by. "I'll text you later."

"Okay," I say. I appreciate that he's saying he's sorry. But I'm still hurt.

I wad my napkin up and take the last sip of my Diet Coke. "I'm going to go," I say. I stand up, not really wanting to get into a fight with Anna, but not wanting to let her off the hook either. It's one thing for Nico to mess around with me—he's a stupid, clueless boy who already has something against Penn—but it's another thing for Anna to do it.

"Harper, come on," she says, rolling her eyes. "I said I'm sorry."

"It's fine." I shrug, but I can feel the anger dissipating and turning into hurt. Tears poke at the backs of my eyes, and I turn and blink them away. And that's when I see them.

Penn. And Sienna Malcolm. They're sitting at the same table, their legs touching as she licks an ice cream cone. There's a box of chicken nuggets on the table in front of them. Penn grabs for one, and Sienna pushes his hand away playfully.

I turn back toward Anna, and she sees it on my face.

"Harper, I'm sorry. I swear, if I had known it was going to make you this upset, I wouldn't have—"

I shake my head. "It's not you," I say.

"Then what?"

I give a slight nod to the side, over to where Penn and Sienna are sitting. Anna looks, and her eyes widen. "Oh," she says. "Okay." She nods, getting it, finally.

She takes my hand and starts leading me to the parking lot.

The only good part of the whole thing is that we're out of there before Penn has a chance to see me.

Penn

I saw her. I saw Harper, and I'm pretty sure she was upset.

Not that I blame her.

I've been acting like a complete and total asshole.

I kissed her, and then I didn't talk to her for two weeks.

I kept telling myself that I would, that I'd call her or text her, or say hi to her at school, or maybe even show up at her dance studio. But I didn't do any of those things.

After a few days I told myself it was because of my dad. He's still not home, and no one knows where he is. My mom is baking more than ever. But after a few days of that, I realized what it really was.

I was scared. Harper was someone I could get attached to. Someone who would want to talk about things, who might want to get close. And I don't want that. Not now. Probably not ever.

But now, seeing her face like that, all upset, makes me feel like a stake is being driven through my heart.

"You need to buy me more chicken nuggets," Sienna says.

"Oh yeah?" I ask, taking another one. "Why's that?" I'm distracted, watching as Harper's friend Anna leads her toward the parking lot.

"Because you're eating mine!" She reaches over and grabs the nugget out of my hand and pops it into her own mouth. Then she goes back to texting on her phone.

This is about as deep as my conversations with Sienna get, which is probably one of the reasons I like hanging out with her. She doesn't ask questions. Ever. She doesn't care about where I am or who I'm with. She doesn't care if we hook up one night and then I don't call her for a few weeks or if I turn up at her house out of nowhere.

I watch Harper and her friend for a few more seconds, and then before I know what I'm doing, I'm standing up.

"I have to go," I say to Sienna.

She shrugs. "Okay. Call me later if you want."

"Sure."

And then I'm following Harper and Anna down the side-walk.

Their heads are huddled kind of close together, and Harper's talking in a low voice as they walk to Anna's car.

"Hey," I say as I mosey on up. I put on my most charming

voice, the voice that used to get me anything I wanted when I was on the baseball team. I reach out and tug a strand of Harper's hair.

She turns around, shock registering on her face. Well. At least it's not hatred, which I've had my fair share of. "Miss me?" I ask brightly.

It's the wrong thing to say.

Harper's eyes narrow into little slits. Wow. She actually looks quite scary giving me the evil eye like that. Maybe Harper isn't quite as innocent as I thought she was. She looks capable of killing someone right about now.

"What do you want?" Anna asks. She crosses her arms over her chest. Suddenly I'm kind of afraid. Anna looks like the type of girl who might haul off and punch you right in the face.

"Just to talk to Harper," I say.

I'm talking to Anna, but I'm looking at Harper. Harper shakes her head slightly. I'm not sure if she's saying *No, I don't want to talk to you* or if she's just shaking her head in disbelief, like she can't believe I have the nerve to come over here and try to talk to her. Which is kind of an overreaction on her part. I mean, yeah, I didn't call her after kissing her, but still. It's not like I pledged my undying love to her or anything. It was one kiss. But girls are sensitive about that kind of stuff.

"Harper doesn't want to talk to you," Anna says.

I ignore her. I understand that she's looking out for her friend, but the last thing I want to do is start getting into something where I'm communicating with Harper through Anna.

"Harper?" I ask. "Do you want to talk to me?"

She bites her lip, and I can see her considering. Then, finally, she shakes her head.

I'm surprised to find that it cuts through me like a knife. "Why not?" I demand.

She looks at me incredulously. "Are you seriously asking me that?"

"Yeah. Don't you think we should talk?"

"After two weeks? *Now* you want to talk?"

"Yeah." I shrug. "Two weeks isn't that long." It really isn't, when you think about it. Fourteen days? Pfft, that's nothing.

"When you kiss someone it is!" she says.

I glance over at Anna, who's looking at Harper with a shocked look on her face. Okay, so Harper didn't tell her that we kissed. Why not? Did she not like the kiss? The kiss, as far as I'm concerned, was amazing. And I know it wasn't my imagination. I'm a very good kisser. Some would say excellent, even. It's kind of what I'm known for.

"I can explain," I say.

"Explanations are for people who have done something wrong," Anna retorts.

Again I answer her, but I'm looking at Harper. "I *have* done something wrong," I say. And then, before I even know I'm saying it, I whisper, "Please, Harper. Let me explain."

I see her face soften, and then, finally, she nods.

"No." Anna shakes her head. "No. I'm not letting you."

"Anna, it's okay," Harper says. "I'll meet you back at school."

"How are you going to get back there?"

"I'll take her," I say. I have my truck, and Sienna drove her own car.

Anna opens her mouth, like maybe she wants to say something else, but then she thinks better of it. "Fine," she says finally. "But you better text me and let me know you got back to school okay."

"I will."

Anna's looking at me like I'm a serial killer, instead of just some high school boy who kissed a girl and then didn't call her for two weeks.

After one last glare she turns and walks away.

"Wow," I say, turning back to Harper. "Your friend is a little overprotective."

"Not really," she says.

Okay, then. "Hi," I try, giving her a smile.

But she doesn't smile back.

"How've you been?"

"Where's Sienna?" she asks.

"Back at our . . . I mean, at the table."

"You're just going to leave her there?"

"It's not just leaving her there," I say. "She has a car. We didn't drive over together."

"Oh, great," she says sarcastically. "So that's how you justify it?"

I frown. "Justify what?"

"The fact that you're just leaving her!"

"I told you, I'm not leaving her. We drove separately."

She turns and starts to walk toward the school, which makes me confused. "Hey," I say, doubling my stride to catch up with her. "What are you doing?"

"Walking back to school."

"It's too hot to walk back to school," I say. "And besides, you said I could drive you."

"Yeah, well, I changed my mind. I've decided I'm mad at you."

"Really?" I step in front of her and block her path. Then I puff out my lip. "I'm too cute for you to be mad at."

I see the determined look on her face falter just a little bit. And that's when I think maybe I have her. My phone buzzes with a text, and I grab it and look down. Braden.

Dad's home, it says. *In bad shape.*

I sigh. I know what that means. It means Braden wants me to go home and deal with it. But I'm in the middle of something. And so instead of responding like I usually do when Braden texts me the newest catastrophe, I just ignore it and slide my cell into my pocket.

"Who was that?" Harper asks.

"No one."

She turns and starts to walk away again.

"Okay, okay," I say, running to catch up. "It was my brother."

"Your brother?"

"Yeah."

She rolls her eyes. "Right."

"What, you think it was some girl?"

"I don't care if it was." She shrugs.

But I can tell she does care. This is crazy. I hardly know this girl. And yet she's somehow getting under my skin. I don't want her to think I was talking to another girl. Mostly I don't want her to leave.

"Here." I hold my phone out to her as we walk.

"What?"

"Look in my phone. Go ahead. My brother's name is Braden. You'll see that the text came from him."

"I'm not going to look in your phone," she says. "That's ridiculous."

I scroll through until I get to Braden's text, then hold it so Harper can see. She doesn't want to look, but it seems like she can't resist. She reads the text, her eyes moving slowly over the words.

"Where was your dad?" she asks softly.

"I don't know."

She's still looking at the phone, and she licks her lips. "Why is he in bad shape?"

I shrug, not wanting to get into it. "He just is."

She studies me for a moment, and I know it sounds odd, but it's almost like she's seeing me for the first time. It actually makes me a little uncomfortable, and for a moment I feel like I need to get out of here. But I know that if I walk away now,

I'm not going to get a second chance. This *is* my second chance, and Harper didn't even really want to give it to me. There's definitely not going to be a third.

"So," I say, holding my breath. "You want to get out of here?"

"Where will we go?" she asks.

"I don't know," I say honestly. "We could have another picnic."

She grins, and then she says, "Are you going to kiss me again?"

The words coming out of her mouth are so unexpected that at first I'm a little shocked she's flirting with me. But then I can't think about anything but kissing her, and how it felt to hold her close to me.

"Maybe."

She shakes her head. "Then I'm not going with you."

"Why not?"

"Because if you're not going to kiss me, then what's the point of hanging out?"

I smile at her.

She smiles at me.

And then I grab her hand and take her to my truck.

Harper

I don't know why I forgave him. Okay, yes, I do. I forgave him because I wanted to, because I couldn't stand the thought of going another two weeks—no, another two *minutes*—without talking to him.

It was weird. When I was standing there in the stupid McDonald's parking lot, I was determined to stay away from him. I mean, I now had concrete proof he was bad news. He'd kissed me and then blown me off for two weeks—not a text, not a hello, nothing—and then I'd seen him with another girl. And if I knew anything about Sienna Malcolm, the two of them are definitely not just friends. I saw them making out in the hallway last year, the kind of making out that causes a teacher to come along and break it up.

But then Penn showed me that text message from his brother, and it was like . . . I don't know. Like I saw him as a person. A person who had more going on than I'd originally thought. And while it didn't make it okay that he'd blown me off, now it seemed less black and white.

So when he took my hand and brought me over to his truck, I let him.

"Are we skipping school again?" I ask. "Because I'm not sure if I should be skipping school again."

"It's not skipping," he says. "It's just . . . postponing."

"What do you mean, 'postponing'?"

"Well, think about it. Whatever you miss, you have to make up, right? Like, if you're not there for a test or something, then you have to make it up later. So you don't actually *skip* it. You just end up doing it later. So it's really just postponing."

"That's the most ridiculous theory I've ever heard," I say. "It's totally skipping, and you know it."

"Postponing."

"Skipping."

"Semantics."

"Ooh," I tease. "The jock player knows more big words."

"I'm full of surprises." He turns the car on, and the air conditioner starts blasting. "So?" He turns and looks at me. "Where should we go? I'm fine going back to school if that's what you want to do. I don't want to corrupt you."

"I don't let anyone corrupt me," I say defiantly, even though that's pretty much exactly what I'm letting him do. I think about it. I never got caught for skipping with him two weeks ago. But that was probably because they thought I was in the nurse's office. My first class after lunch is math, and Mr. Westwood is a stickler for attendance. If I get caught skipping class, they're probably going to call my mom, and it's probably going to become some big deal.

On the other hand, if I don't go with Penn, then I don't know when I'm going to see him again. Yes, he seems sincere. But what if he disappears again for two weeks like he did before? It's confusing.

I bite my lip and think about it.

And then I say, "Let's go somewhere."

The Southboro Field Days are going on in the center of town, and so that's where Penn takes me. The SFDs used to have something to do with May Day, or Cinco de Mayo or something, but at some point over the years they just sort of morphed into a random event in May.

There are carnival games and rides and cotton candy and a psychic named Madame Sashi, who's definitely not psychic, because last year she told me I was going to move to India and work with aquatic animals. I tried to tell her that unless Ballard University decided to relocate to India, and unless working with aquatic animals was a new kind of choreography, she was wrong. But Madame Sashi didn't listen. In fact, she was kind of insistent. So insistent that when Anna asked her to refund my five dollars, her assistant ushered us out of the tent and told us not to come back.

Anyway, today's the first day of the field days, and they just opened at noon. But even though the Southboro Field Days are kind of a big deal in our town, most people go at night, so there's hardly anyone here right now. It's mostly just moms with little kids. We walk around a bit, and then Penn buys me some fried dough.

"So are we going to talk about this?" I ask as we weave our way through the booths. I rip off a piece of fried dough and pop it into my mouth, letting the sweetness slide over my taste buds. Technically it's still spring, but it feels like summer, so I pull off my hoodie and tie it around my waist.

"About what?" Penn asks.

"About how you kissed me and then didn't call me for two weeks?"

"I said I was sorry."

"Yeah, but . . ." Something inside me feels like I'm owed more explanation. *But you aren't. You guys aren't even together. You hung out a little bit and then he kissed you. He didn't make you any promises. He didn't say he was going to call you.* That was all true. In fact, all he said when he left that night was "See you tomorrow," and he *did* see me at school the next day. He hadn't said "*Talk* to you tomorrow" or "Text you later" or anything like that.

And it was just a kiss. Well, more like a make-out session. But still.

"Yeah," I say. "But . . . why didn't you call me?"

He shrugs. "I had shit going on." His eyes are dark, and his face takes on a blank expression. It's the same expression he had the other day when we ran into Jackson at the batting cages. I'm starting to realize it's the expression he gets when he shuts down and doesn't want to talk about something.

"Okay." I eat another piece of fried dough, but this one somehow doesn't taste as sweet. I know I'm being crazy. I know I should just let it go. But I can't.

"Let me make it up to you," Penn says, nodding toward one of the carnival booths. It's one of those games where you throw a baseball and try to knock over a pyramid of milk bottles. There are all different kinds of stuffed animal prizes hanging from the ceiling—pink puppies and yellow giraffes and baby-blue koala bears.

"You wanna play?" the red-haired kid running the game asks. He's wearing a striped porkpie hat and a neon-green shirt that says CARNY across the front. He tosses one of the baseballs up into the air and then catches it.

"Yeah." Penn rummages around in his pocket.

"It's a dollar for one ball or three dollars for five," the kid says.

"Just one." Penn plunks a dollar down onto the wooden railing that goes around the perimeter of the booth. "That's all it's gonna take."

"You have to knock down all three milk jugs," the kid says doubtfully. "And you have to do it with one throw."

113

"Yeah, I know how the game works," Penn says.

The kid shrugs and hands Penn a baseball.

Penn squints at the pyramid of milk bottles, draws his throwing arm back, and lets loose. The ball hits right in the middle of the stack, and the bottle on top immediately clatters onto the wooden floor. The bottom right one falls next. And the last bottle totters for a second while we all stand there holding our breath. It balances on its edge, about to fall over, and then at the last second rights itself.

"Oooh," the carnie says, snapping his fingers. "So close. I told ya you should've gotten those other balls."

Penn doesn't say anything. He smiles at the kid, but I can tell he's not really amused.

"That's okay," I say, trying to defuse the situation. "No big deal. I really don't have any place to put a giant unicorn anyway." It's true. I've always thought stuffed animals were kind of stupid, even when I was at an age when stuffed animals were appropriate. I was never the kind of kid who had tons of them on her bed or anything like that. And besides, my room is a mess on its best day.

"Give me another ball," Penn says, pulling out a fresh dollar. He slams it down onto the wooden railing instead of handing it to the kid, almost like he's making some kind of statement.

The kid looks at the dollar doubtfully. "You sure you don't want to do the five for three this time?"

"I'm sure," Penn says.

The kid sighs like he's seen this all before, and then takes the money.

I figure Penn will take more time to set up his shot, but it's the opposite. It's like his body switches into autopilot, and he doesn't even think or aim or anything. He just throws the ball. A second later all three bottles go toppling to the ground.

I didn't realize I was so invested in what was about to happen, until I hear myself shout out, "Yes!"

Penn turns around and grins, then picks me up and twirls me around. His arms around my waist make me feel tiny, and the fact that he's picking me up like it's nothing is sexy.

Before he sets me down, he kisses me quickly on the lips. It's not as intense as it was when he kissed me at the park, but somehow it's better. He's doing it here, in public, where everyone can see. Not that anyone we know is at the field days. Everyone's in school. But still.

"What stuffed animal do you want?" the carny asks Penn.

Penn turns and looks at me, and I glance up at the prizes. There's a huge teddy bear that's pretty cute, and a medium-size spotted dog with floppy ears. "I'll take the dog," I say.

The carny reaches up with this hook thing, pulls the dog down, and then hands it to me. I know I said I didn't want it, but suddenly I've never been so excited to have a stuffed animal in my life. I stroke its fur, wondering if it would be taking it too far to give my new dog a name. I always wanted a dog named Gizmo.

"I've never seen anyone win on their second try," the carny

says to Penn. "Or even the third or fourth. You play ball?"

I expect Penn to stiffen like he does whenever anyone brings up baseball, but instead he just shrugs. "Used to."

The carny nods, and then suddenly his eyes light up with recognition. "Hey, I know you," he says. "You're Penn Mattingly!" A second later his excited expression turns to one of regret. "Dude, sorry about your arm. I think it's fucked up that Duke would just drop you like that. I'll bet if you hadn't gotten hurt, you would have gone pro."

"Yeah, maybe," Penn says, but he's already turning and walking away.

I run to catch up with him, trying not to drop my stuffed dog. It's not like it has a handle or anything, so I've got my arms around its middle, which definitely isn't conducive to maneuvering through a crowd.

Where did all these people come from? I wonder as I dodge through a bunch of them, almost knocking over a toddler. Just a second ago it was completely dead around here.

"Hey!" I yell to Penn. I'm starting to lose sight of him in the crowd.

"Look at the girl with the stuffed animal, Mommy!" a little girl yells. "I want a stuffed animal like that for my room! Why does that big girl get it when stuffed animals are for little girls?"

I rush by as quickly as I can, not really liking being called a big girl. I know she meant older, but still.

To my relief Penn stops to wait for me near the snow

cone machine, where there's a break in the crowd. But once I catch up with him, he takes the dog out of my hands and then starts walking even faster toward the car.

"Hello?" I ask him. "What are you doing?"

"Going to the car," he says matter-of-factly, like that was the plan all along, and we didn't just get to the carnival, oh, I don't know, five minutes ago.

"Oh, okay," I say. "That makes sense. You know, since we got here, like, five minutes ago."

He doesn't reply. When we get to his car, he opens one of the back doors and sets Gizmo down gently on the seat. Which is kind of weird. Penn's obviously in a bad mood, you can tell, so the fact that he sets my dog down so carefully is crazy.

I get into the car, and then *he* gets into the car, and then we just sit there.

After a moment I glance at him out of the corner of my eye.

His elbow is resting against the door, his hand cupping his chin. He's just gazing out the window, not saying anything. He doesn't look mad, but he doesn't look *not* mad, either.

I don't say anything, wondering how the mood changed so quickly. Again I'm reminded of when we were at the batting cages, and I bite my lip.

"So," I say. "Um . . . are we . . . I mean, are you going to take me home now or . . ."

"Why, do you *want* to go home?"

"Well, kind of, if you're going to act like that."

He lets out a sigh, then reaches over and grabs my hand.

"I'm sorry, Harper," he says. "I just . . . I'm moody."

"Yeah, ya think?"

He grins, and just like that, he's back to his old self. "Yeah. It's a character flaw." He winks. "My only one, actually."

He goes to start the car again, but I reach out and put my hand on his. "No."

"No?" He frowns. "You want to go back to the carnival?"

I shake my head. "I want you to tell me why you flipped out and got all weird. Was it because of what that kid said? About your arm?"

I can tell it's his instinct to shake his head, but he must change his mind because a second later he swallows hard and takes a deep breath. Finally he nods. "I don't like when people recognize me."

"From baseball, you mean?"

"Yeah."

"Why not?"

He shrugs. "Because they feel sorry for me. And I hate that."

"That makes sense," I say slowly. I twist my hands in my lap and think about it. "But, Penn, that guy at the carnival doesn't even know you."

"So?"

"So his opinion doesn't matter."

He laughs like this is the funniest thing he's ever heard. "Really, Harper?" he asks. "You've never worried about what someone you didn't know thought of you?"

"I didn't say that."

"Yes, you did."

"No, I didn't."

"Yes, you did. You said his opinion didn't matter."

"It doesn't."

He shakes his head. "We're talking in circles."

"Okay." I bite my lip again and don't say anything. I don't know why he's getting so upset, and it's crazy that we're having what could kind of be considered a fight, when we're not even together.

"I'm sorry," he says again.

"It's okay." But I'm not sure if it is. I wonder why I'm even here, dealing with this. Penn's angsty and secretive, and he blew me off for two weeks. I could be doing a million other more productive things right now. I think about these past weeks, all the time I wasted hoping he was going to call. Time I could have spent doing schoolwork, or hanging out with Anna, or working on my piece for my Ballard choreography audition. And suddenly I don't want to be here anymore. It's like my head's been fighting my heart, and finally my head's like, *Okay, that's enough!* and pushes my heart right out of the way.

"I think," I say finally, "that you should bring me home."

Penn

What can I do? I bring her home.

I know I'm acting like a jerk, but how am I supposed to explain it? I don't want to talk about it. I don't want to even *feel* it. If I let myself, it's only going to bring up a whole host of other things, things I'm definitely not ready to deal with.

When I pull into Harper's driveway, she says, "Thanks so much for a fun afternoon," all sarcastic like, before getting out of the car and slamming the door behind her.

I watch her walk up the sidewalk, and then I realize it's still the middle of the day, so I roll down the window and say, "Hey, you do realize you're supposed to be at school, right?"

But she doesn't answer me.

And then she disappears into her house. An internal

struggle starts inside me over whether or not I should go after her. I'm about to turn off my car and go to the door, but what would I say? I already apologized, and apparently that wasn't good enough. And there's no way I'm going to be able to get into all my fucked up shit with her in the span of a few minutes. I don't even want to.

Besides, we're supposed to be at school. And her mom is obviously not a big fan of me after what happened the other night at the dance studio. So after a second I pull out of the driveway.

There's a stop sign at the end of her street, and I stop there for a second and turn my cell phone back on. There are three more texts from my brother, along with a voicemail from Dr. Marzetti's office in Boston.

I hold my breath as I listen to the message, but it's the same thing they always say. That they're not taking new patients, that they have an extremely long wait list but that they'll put me on it, and if anything opens up in the next six months or so, they'll let me know.

I let my breath out and try not to feel disappointment. Six months from now might as well be a lifetime. Six months is too late. In six months everything will be over. Every scholarship will be given out. Everyone will already know where they're going to school, everyone will have their futures set, and I'll be stuck here with no one but Braden and my parents.

I don't know why I even bother to let Dr. Marzetti's office call me. Back when I first got hurt, my dad gave them a call and put me on some list (this was during one of his lucid, non-drinking months), and now they call periodically to give me updates.

Not like it matters. The only way I'd even have a chance at playing college ball is if I somehow got better by the end of the summer. Which is a complete long shot. I can't even get an appointment with this Dr. Marzetti, much less know if she can help me. She's supposed to be a miracle worker, but that doesn't mean anything. Even miracle workers have their limits.

If I was from a rich family, or if I had a high-powered coach who would vouch for me, I probably could get in sooner. But I'm not and I don't. So every month they leave a message and tell me I'm on the waiting list and that they'll let me know if they have a cancellation. But they're never going to have a cancellation, because no one's going to cancel an appointment that's ridiculously hard to get in the first place.

Whatever. It's not like I give a shit.

I scroll through the texts from my brother, which are pretty much all the same—different variations of asking me when I'm coming home, telling me that my dad is doing better, etc., etc.

I'm in a sour mood, so I decide, fuck it, why not go home? I'm already pissed off. How can things get any worse?

So I turn my truck around.

When I get there, my dad's car is in the driveway, parked at an odd angle. The headlights are on, and I shake my head, annoyed, mostly at my brother. Braden should have known he needed to check the car and make sure everything was turned off. But he was probably too high to think of it, or maybe he expected I'd take care of it when I got home.

When I walk into the house, I expect to see my dad zoned out on his favorite recliner, maybe nursing a coffee or flipping through the channels.

Instead my whole family is sitting at the dining room table.

"Penn!" my mom says when she sees me. Her eyes light up like a Christmas tree. "We're so glad you're here! Come sit. I made lunch."

I gape at her. "Don't you want to know why I'm not at school?" I ask.

"I know why you're not at school." She reaches out and squeezes Braden's arm. "Because you came home as soon as Braden called you."

I glance over at my dad. He's sitting there with a plate full of food in front of him, shoveling what looks like spaghetti into his mouth. "Hey, Penn," he says happily. "Come sit down, buddy. Have some food."

This is where things get weird. You'd expect that since I'm already in a bad mood, and my dad has basically disappeared for a few weeks and then just randomly decided to come home, that I'd tell him to fuck off and then I'd turn around and leave. Not to mention the fact that my brother and mother are acting like my dad's behavior is totally fine. Obviously my mom left work in the middle of the day, and for what? To serve my dad a huge Italian lunch in the hopes that this time he'll stick around?

The whole situation is completely and totally bizarre.

But I don't tell them to fuck off, I don't tell them how crazy they are. I don't even turn around and walk out. Instead I sit down.

My mom gets up and bustles around the kitchen and returns with a full plate of food for me.

I look down at it, then pick up my fork and start to eat.

Braden's plate is already empty. He's a big eater, and not just because he's always high. He just loves food. He reaches for the basket of bread on the table, pulls out a hunk, and then rips off a crust before dragging it through the sauce that's left on his plate.

"You should see the fence the McCarthys are putting in next door," my mom says to my dad. She sets another piece of bread on his plate, and he picks it up and starts to butter it. "It's horrendous. Do you think you could talk to them?"

"Sure," my dad says, taking a bite of his bread. "Bill's always been a reasonable guy."

"Well, it's probably Wendy who wanted it," my mom says. "That woman absolutely loves buying things that are gaudy. Have you seen her great room?" My mom starts prattling on about all our neighbor's knickknacks. My dad listens and eats his bread, shaking his head and laughing as my mom tells jokes. My brother is just sitting there, reading texts on his phone.

"I have to go," Braden says, standing up. "I'm meeting Austin."

Austin is Braden's only real friend. That's because most of Braden's other friends are away at college, and the ones who aren't have jobs. But Austin's a burnout just like Braden. Not that college kids don't smoke pot—I know plenty of them who do—but Austin takes it to a whole other level. He's baked constantly, and I'm pretty sure he deals, too.

"Have fun, honey," my mom says.

I wonder what she would say if I told her that I know for a fact Austin got arrested last year for selling OxyContin, and that if Braden is hanging out with him, it's probably only a matter of time before he gets arrested himself.

"Do you want more spaghetti?" my mom asks me.

I look down at my plate, surprised to see that I've eaten almost everything on it. But this is how it usually is when my family is all together. It's hard to explain, but it's like I go on autopilot. I start playing a character in a movie—the Dutiful Son. The Dutiful Son sits and eats and doesn't make waves. Meanwhile, the whole time I feel this really strange disconnect from my body, almost like I'm not supposed to be there, like I'm not supposed to be doing this. It's sort of like being in a dream.

"No, thanks," I say. "I have . . . I mean, I'm going to the batting cages." That wasn't my plan. But suddenly it's like a switch has flipped and I need to get out of here. I thought I'd be coming home to help my dad into bed, to brew him coffee and set up a trash can near him in case he needed to be sick. But apparently he's somehow skipped all that, and we've fast-forwarded to the part of the process I hate the most—the part where everyone pretends everything is fine.

My dad shakes his head. "No point in that, Penn."

"What?" I ask.

"No point in going to the batting cages." He chews on his lip and then takes a sip of his water. "Baseball's over for you, Son. And the quicker you accept that, the better off you'll be."

My mom instantly becomes nervous. She reaches for the wooden salad bowl and begins spooning salad onto my plate. Which makes no sense, since my plate had spaghetti on it. The lettuce falls into the sauce. "Have some salad before you go," she babbles. "You know you need to have your veggies, Penn. It's very important."

"Just because I'm not getting a scholarship doesn't mean I can't go to the batting cages." My hands start to clench my napkin. My body feels like it's pulled tight, almost like a high-tension wire, but my voice sounds surprisingly calm.

My dad shrugs. "But what's the point? It's a waste of time. You need to focus on your schoolwork. Otherwise you're going to end up working at McDonald's."

"A waste of time?" I laugh. You'd think it would be a bitter sound, but it's not. In fact, my laugh sounds like I really am trying to make a funny joke. "Kind of like going out and drinking for days?"

"Penn!" my mom gasps. I've broken the one rule of our house. The rule that states that under no circumstances is anyone ever allowed to bring up the fact that my dad has a drinking problem. "Apologize to your father right now!"

"No."

"No!" She repeats it, but it's not a question. It's like she's in shock.

"It's fine, Patricia," my dad says. "Penn's always been stubborn. Which is why he's going to the batting cages. He still can't accept the truth."

I'm gripping the napkin so hard now that I can feel my nails digging into my skin through the cloth. My dad has no idea what he's talking about. He has no idea about what I have or haven't accepted. He hasn't been around. If he had been, then maybe he'd know that the only time I go to the batting cages is when I can't take it anymore, when the need to play baseball wells up inside me so hard that it becomes unbearable. That the only time I truly forget about everything that's going on, with Braden, with my dad, with my family, with my injury—is when I'm hitting that ball. And even though that's true, I still don't ever let myself hit it that hard, with my full power, because I'm scared to death that if I do, I'm going to hurt my shoulder even more.

I want to say all those things to my dad, but I don't trust myself. If I go there, the anger that's sure to bubble up inside me isn't going to be controllable.

"I'm leaving." I wipe my mouth and stand up from the table. My voice still sounds surprisingly calm.

"Are you sure?" my mom asks, like she didn't just yell at me a second before. "I made an Oreo pie for dessert."

"No, thanks."

I head outside.

I start to drive to the batting cages, but once I'm at the sports complex, I spot Jackson's car sitting in the parking lot. The last thing I want is to run into Jackson. I'm so tightly wound right now that if I see him, there's a good chance I'll end up popping him in the face.

I drive around for a while, not doing much of anything. I stop and buy a coffee at a drive-through Dunkin' Donuts. I do a loop around town, taking back roads and avoiding highways. Eventually I find myself in front of Harper's house. But her car's not in the driveway.

I glance at the clock. It's three. She's probably at work.

So I turn my truck around. And somehow, before I know it, I'm at Harper's mom's dance studio.

The exterior sign is lit up, and there are huge floor-to-ceiling windows lining the parking lot. I can see a few couples in there dancing. One of the women is wearing a long white dress, and her skirt flows as she dances. Something about it is weirdly comforting.

I sit there for a second, not sure what I'm doing. Am I going inside? And if so, why? That's stalkerish. Besides, I was a complete asshole to her. There's no way she's going to want to see me.

I start to put my car into reverse and get the hell out of here, but when the car moves backward, the pavement goes up on a gradient and the engine of my truck revs. Harper's mom looks up, and her eyes meet mine.

Shit. I'm not sure if she saw me. There's no way she saw me, right? And even if she did, there's no way she would recognize me. I mean, I've only met her once.

But now Harper's mom is crossing the room and she's opening the door, and she's peering out into the parking lot.

She's definitely seen me now. Why didn't I pull out of here when I had the chance? I thought peeling out would have looked way more insane, but now I wish I'd just hightailed it out. Who cares if Harper's mom thinks I'm insane? Harper already thinks I'm insane, and honestly, who cares if she does? She's just a girl that I kissed one time, a girl that I was a jerk to, a girl that I—

"Who's there?" Harper's mom calls, which makes no sense. Why would she be so upset about a car being in the parking lot? Unless, of course, she knows it's me.

I grit my teeth and pull the car back into the parking spot. Now that she's caught me, I guess there's nothing I can really do. Except maybe some damage control. From what I saw of her the other day, she seems like the real uptight type. The kind of person who would call the police if she saw a strange teenage boy just sitting in the parking lot of her dance studio.

I get out of the car and paste an innocent look on my face, like I'm not doing anything wrong and it's totally normal for me to be sitting here. And why isn't it? Me and Harper are friends. Well, if you count people who kiss and then have a fight and then show up at someone's mother's dance studio hoping to see them as friends.

"Oh, hi," I say, stepping out of the car. "It's nice to see you again." I'm not sure what I should call her. Harper's dad is out of the picture, so I don't want to be presumptuous and call her mom Mrs. Fairbanks if that's not her name. She looks me up and down, then cocks her head to one side like she's thinking about whether or not I'm worthy of a response.

"Penn, right?" she asks.

I nod. "Yes."

We just stand there for a moment. It's actually kind of weird, because it's very awkward out here, and yet you can hear this sort of sexy dance music trailing out from inside into the parking lot.

"Um, is Harper here?" I ask finally.

"Yes."

I wait for her to go get Harper, or to at least move aside so I can go into the studio, but she doesn't. She just stands there, looking formidable.

"Can I see her?" I try.

"I don't know if she wants to see you right now."

Great. So Harper's mom knows about our fight. For a moment I consider pretending I don't know what she's talking about, or maybe just turning around and walking away. I mean, talking to some girl's mom about the fight you got into with her daughter? This is exactly why I don't ever get involved in emotional relationships. It's too messy.

But something stops me from leaving. "She told you what happened?"

Harper's mom nods.

Then I nod.

I think about it. And for the first time in a long time, I don't worry about what I should say, or how I should be feeling, or anything stupid like that. Instead I just say, "Do you think she might want to hear me apologize?"

Harper's mom shrugs. "I'm not sure." It's actually kind of disconcerting, hearing her say that. She doesn't seem like the kind of woman who ever isn't sure about anything.

"Well, can I try?"

She looks right into my eyes, and I swear it's like some kind of test or something. She's suspicious of me. She doesn't know if I'm good for her daughter. And I don't blame her. Hell, *I* don't even know if I'm good for her daughter.

But maybe she sees something in me I didn't know was there, or maybe she's just sick of standing outside, but the next thing I know, she's nodding. I move past her into the dance studio.

I can see Harper through the glass partition that encloses the office. She's typing away on the computer. When she sees me, her face sort of brightens, but then a second later it darkens again.

I give her a wave, and she hesitates. Then, finally, she gets up out of her chair and enters the studio.

"Hi," she says.

"Hi." Now that I'm here and she's talking to me, I'm relieved. I didn't realize how much I wanted her to not be mad at me. I take a step toward her and smile. "You working?"

She nods.

"How much longer?"

"I'm done at eight."

"You want to get out of here after?"

Her face goes back to that sort of confused expression. I hold my breath and wait for her answer.

Harper

He's here! Penn's here to see me!

I know it's totally ridiculous and pathetic, since he was just a complete asshole to me earlier, but I'm happy. I'd been having this awful feeling that it was going to be two weeks before I talked to him again, and even though I was telling myself it was okay if I didn't talk to him for two weeks because he was a complete douchebag, I wasn't really being that convincing.

All I could think about was how much I wanted to see him, how it had felt to kiss him, how he'd won me a dumb stuffed animal. And then I started getting this strange feeling that I wasn't going to see him ever again, which was stupid, because obviously I'm going to see him again at school. I see him pretty much every *day* at school. But that's different.

I meant *see him* see him, like kiss him and hold his hand and let his hands wander all over—

No, I tell myself. *I must not let my hormones and crazy girl thoughts start to run wild. I need to play it cool.*

"I don't think we should hang out," I say. It's a ploy. I want him to convince me.

"Why not?"

"Because you ditched me earlier."

He looks confused. "I didn't ditch you."

"Yes, you did. You got all upset and then you left me."

"I didn't *leave* you. I brought you home, safe and sound."

I shake my head. "Are you just going to keep denying everything I say? You're totally discounting my feelings."

Out of the corner of my eye, I can see my mom watching us from across the room. She's supposed to be giving Jeremy and Kaitlyn a dance lesson, but she seems much more interested in me and Penn.

"Discounting your feelings?" Penn asks. "What are you talking about?"

"Look, I don't think we should get into this here." The last thing I want to do is start some big thing in front of everyone at the dance studio. There's enough drama here.

"Good idea," he says, giving me that maddening grin that makes me want to melt. "Let's get out of here. After you're done working, of course. I've corrupted you enough for the day."

I shake my head, trying not to smile. I'm mad at him. "I can't go out with you after work."

"I need to be forgiven." He puffs his lip out in this totally adorable way. "What can I do?"

"To be forgiven?"

"Yeah."

I think about it. But before I can decide on anything, he leans in so close to me that his cheek brushes against mine. "I'll make it up to you," he says, "if you come out with me later. I promise."

His voice sounds dark and dangerous and vaguely threatening. But in a sexy way. Like he's making a promise that he's going to follow through on. He pauses there for a moment, not moving, not saying anything, just letting the anticipation linger in the air. A little shiver moves up my spine.

"Okay," I say. "Meet me outside at eight."

By the time the dance studio is closing, my hormones have calmed down. Sort of.

"So," I say to my mom after I shut down my computer and lock up the office. "I'm going out for a little while, but I'll see you at home later?"

She's still working with Jeremy and Kaitlyn, who are having some kind of argument over whether or not it's appropriate for someone to wear a pink wedding dress.

"The wedding dress is supposed to reflect what the bride wants to wear," Kaitlyn is saying. "It's the most important thing about the whole day!"

"The bride can wear whatever she wants if she's paying for

it," Jeremy says. "But if she's not, and the groom's mother is paying, then the groom's mother is expecting to see the bride in white."

"Well, the groom's mother wouldn't have to pay if the *groom* hadn't quit his job to become a stand-up comedian." Kaitlyn plops down onto a chair, then pulls off one of her dance shoes and gestures wildly with it. "Seriously! A stand-up comedian! Have you ever heard of anything so ridiculous?"

She's looking at me, but I'm not sure if she's really talking to me, and I'm not sure if she even wants an answer. But then she sort of tilts her head expectantly, so I say, "Um, well, if it's his dream . . ."

"Thank you!" Jeremy says. "It *is* my dream. It's been my dream ever since I was a little kid. And if you want to start talking about crazy dreams, maybe we should talk about the fact that you ran through half of our savings starting Kaitlyn's Cupcakes!"

Kaitlyn's face darkens, and for a moment I'm afraid she's going to throw her shoe across the room at Jeremy. "I knew you were going to bring that up! You said we had the money! And it wasn't my fault the crates of sprinkles melted. How was I supposed to know they needed to be refrigerated?"

"Oh, I don't know," Jeremy says. He reaches over and takes the shoe out of her hand, then puts it into her dance bag. "Maybe because they're chocolate? And chocolate melts in heat!"

"Okay!" my mom says brightly. "So we'll see you two tomorrow, then?"

They don't answer her and instead head toward the door, bickering the whole way.

I'm kind of sad to see them go. One, because they're way more interesting than the older people we usually get in here, and two, because there's no way my mom would feel like she could ask me tons of questions about where I'm going and who I'm going with if there were other people around.

"So I'll text you later," I say brightly, and start walking toward the door.

"Stop!" my mom calls. She walks over to me. My mom and I have never really talked about things like boys and relationships, so the fact that I told her about what happened with Penn earlier just shows how much he's gotten under my skin. Now, though, I realize what a mistake it was confiding in her. I really don't want to get into this.

"Yeah?" I turn around and then pull my phone out of my bag and start looking down at it, like I'm so nonchalant about going out with Penn that I can just text while I'm getting ready to leave, la, la, la.

"I want to meet him."

"Mom." I roll my eyes. "You don't have to meet him. It's not even a thing. Besides, you already met him, remember?"

"You're going out with him on a school night. And you were obviously upset about him earlier."

I curse myself again for telling her about what happened at the carnival. But when I came into work, it was impossible to hide it. She asked me what happened, and I gave her an abridged version. She was actually very cool about the whole thing—she didn't even say anything about me skipping school.

"I wasn't *upset*," I say. "I was just annoyed."

"You seemed upset. You *said* you were upset."

Did I say that? I can't remember. "Well, I'm over it now," I say. "Aren't you always telling me not to overanalyze things? That I need to just relax and let everything be breezy?"

My mom frowns and looks at me like maybe I'm a little crazy. "No." She shakes her head. "I don't remember ever saying that to you."

"Well, you should have," I say, putting my phone back into my bag. "I'm obviously, you know, wound very tight."

My mom's face darkens. "Is that what this boy is telling you? That you're wound tight?" She crosses her arms over her chest. "Is he pressuring you in any way?" She looks out the window to where Penn is sitting in his truck, drumming his fingers on the steering wheel to whatever song he's listening to. I catch my breath again at just how cute he is. My mom is glaring at him. "Harper, sex is a very important—"

"Mom!" I say, cutting her off. "I know that! And he's not pressuring me."

"Are you sure?" She's still giving Penn the evil eye through the window, like she's half expecting him to come in here and just start ripping my clothes off.

"I'm sure!"

She relaxes her shoulders. The CD that's been on in the studio, a slow mix of rumba songs, stops playing, and there's just silence now. I'm not sure what to say.

My mom apparently thinks Penn is some kind of sex-crazed maniac. And actually, now that I think about it, do I really know that he's not? I mean, he kissed me the very first night we hung out. And it's not like Sienna Malcolm has the best reputation. Not that there's anything wrong with having sex. But I don't know if—

"Still," my mom says, breaking into my thoughts. "I should meet him. If he's going to be driving you around tonight, I should meet him. Properly."

I start to open my mouth to protest, but I can see the look in her eye. It's the look she gets when she's not going to back down from something. I take in a big deep breath and let it out.

"Fine," I grumble. "I'll go get him."

I push through the front doors of the dance studio, wondering if there's any way Penn is going to refuse to come in and meet my mom. I knock on the driver-side door, and he lowers the music and then rolls down the window.

"Hey, cutie," he says sexily. Oh God. His voice sounds all hot and melty, the kind of voice that makes you want to cuddle up and lose your senses.

"Hi," I say.

"You ready?"

"Ready for what?" Jesus, now my mom's got me thinking all sorts of crazy things about Penn's intentions. The most innocent things he's saying are making me have all kinds of bad thoughts. I take a deep breath. I'm totally overthinking this. I really am wound tight, it turns out. Penn is being completely normal, and I need to just calm down.

"Ready for whatever," he says, this time even sexier. Okay, so maybe he's not so innocent.

"So the thing is," I say, "is that my mom wants to meet you."

"I already met her." He glances toward the dance studio, where my mom is trying to pretend like she's going over Kaitlyn and Jeremy's dance notes and not stealing glances at me and Penn through the window.

If he looks like he's putting up a fight, or doesn't want to do it, she's probably going to be that much harder on him. I take a few steps to the side, making sure to block her view so that if he does give me a hard time, she won't be able to tell.

"Yeah, I know," I say. "But she probably wants to talk and get to know you a little bit more."

"Why?" He doesn't say it in a smart-ass way. He sounds like he really does want to know.

"Because you're going to be driving me around, and she gets uncomfortable with me being driven by people she doesn't know." I'm definitely not going to mention the fact that she thinks he's a sex maniac. I want them to get along, and I don't think that would start them off on the right foot.

"You go out with strange guys a lot?"

"No!" I say automatically, before realizing I probably protested too quickly. I mean, why shouldn't I go out with strange guys? I don't want Penn to think that while he was busy ignoring me for two weeks, I was sitting at home crying. He should be thinking that I was out with random men, dancing the night away and doing other scandalous things. Of course, any men who were really that strange and dangerous probably wouldn't have consented to coming in to meet my mom, so I wouldn't have been able to go out with them anyway. "I mean, sometimes I do. I mean, not a lot, but, you know."

He smiles and shakes his head, like he's onto my game. Then he reaches over and turns the engine off. He swings his long legs out onto the pavement. "Okay," he says, and shrugs. "Let's get this over with."

It goes better than planned. Except for one extremely awkward moment when my mom asks Penn if he plays any sports, and Penn gets all broody and says "no," and then my mom asks him if he's one of those guys who thinks that all people who play sports are preppy losers, and then Penn has to explain that no, he doesn't think that, he used to play baseball until he got injured.

And then my mom starts to ask him what happened, and Penn sort of shuts down, and then I have to say that he's still working on maybe getting his shoulder fixed, but that it's getting late, and so we should probably leave.

So then my mom kind of relaxes and is like, "Okay. Well, have a good time."

When we get to the car, Penn's all quiet.

"Your mom asks a lot of questions," he says finally.

I shrug. "She's just a mom."

He shakes his head. "*My* mom doesn't even ask me questions like that."

I look at him, surprised. "Really?"

"Really."

"She doesn't care who you're seeing or what you're doing?"

His face hardens a little, and then he shakes his head. "So," he says, "what should we do?"

I swallow. I don't know what I want to do. Actually, that's not really true. I do know what I want to do. I want him to take me somewhere. Not to some rinky-dink batting cages, not to some stupid carnival in the middle of the day, not to some park where we sit and things get all weird.

I want to go somewhere real.

"Take me somewhere real," I say.

"What's that supposed to mean?"

I shrug. "You know, like somewhere normal."

"You mean like a date?" He sounds sort of shocked, like the thought never occurred to him.

I nod.

"Okay," he says slowly, and then smiles. "The Sailing Burrito?"

"Great." I settle back in my seat. The Sailing Burrito is perfect. But for some reason my stomach does a flip, and a feeling of trepidation rises up and into my throat. But I push it right back down. I mean, it's just dinner. What could happen?

Penn

This is definitely a mistake. Somehow I have agreed to take Harper out to the Sailing Burrito. The Sailing Burrito is this Mexican place that's close to our school. It's only open for dinner, and the food there is pretty disgusting.

But at night everyone from our school shows up there. It's almost like a big cafeteria, with everyone moving from one table to the next. When it's warm out, like it is tonight, they open up their huge outdoor patio. I guess the original idea was that the patio would be used mostly for happy hours—they'd play music and serve piña coladas and daiquiris. But almost immediately after the place opened, the high school kids started to take over, and after a while the owner kind of just went with it. The food isn't really good enough to attract the after-work crowd, and so now everyone from school hangs out there and drinks virgin margaritas on the deck.

Showing up with Harper is kind of like making a public declaration. It's like a declaration that we're . . . not together, but at least, you know, *together*.

I look over at her. She's twirling a strand of hair around her finger, her head tilted slightly as she looks out the window.

All those questions her mom was asking threw me. Who asks questions like that? Especially the one about how she could be sure I wasn't going to leave her daughter tonight the way I had earlier at the carnival. I mean, really? How was I supposed to answer that? And why did Harper tell her mom about that anyway? God, she's so sexy, though.

I watch as she pulls her leg up onto the seat and sort of leans her chin against her knee, and I so want to kiss her. Her hair falls over her face in soft waves, and I resist the urge to reach over and run my fingers through it. Her T-shirt hugs her in just the right places. I shift on the seat and try to keep my thoughts a little more innocent. But she smells so damn good that it's difficult.

"You're being quiet," I say. "Don't you want to talk?" I need something to keep my mind off the impure thoughts running through my head.

"Yes." She turns to me and pushes her hair behind her ear, and I notice she's wearing sparkly purple flip-flops. Her feet are tan, and her toenails are painted light purple. "Let's talk about how you freaked out earlier and ditched me."

"I didn't ditch you."

"Yes, you did."

"No. 'Ditching' would mean that I left you at the carnival. Which I most certainly did not. I dropped you off at home, safe and sound."

She shakes her head. "'Ditching' means that you left me. 'Stranding me' would be if you left me at the carnival."

I roll my eyes and pull into the parking lot of the Sailing Burrito. We have to pass by the deck to find a spot, and the place is packed. I shut off the engine, pull the keys out of the ignition, and flip them around my finger. "You ready?" I ask.

"Yup." She unhooks her seat belt and opens the car door.

As we're walking across the parking lot, Harper does this little skip thing, almost like a little kid, and it's so adorable that before I know what I'm doing, I reach out and grab her hand.

I see her sort of stiffen in surprise, but then she turns and looks at me and gives me a smile, and Jesus Christ, how did I stay away from her for two whole weeks? This shouldn't be happening. This shouldn't be working. We're so different. She's this innocent, smart, beautiful girl, and I'm just . . . I don't know exactly what I am.

I used to. But I don't anymore.

We head into the restaurant, still holding hands, but when we get inside, I feel suddenly exposed, like showing up here with Harper is making a statement I'm not sure I'm ready for. It's an overwhelming feeling, and so I drop her hand. I make sure not to look over at her while I do it, because I'm not going to be able to take it if she seems disappointed.

Miraculously we somehow find a table over on the far side of the deck. There are a bunch of paper lanterns strung up on the wall, and the light shines down and illuminates Harper's face.

"You hungry?" I ask, picking up one of the paper menus that are on every table.

"Yeah, kind of."

"Kind of?"

She smiles. "I am hungry, but I don't know if I'm hungry enough to actually eat the food here."

"We can get piña coladas. And the chips usually aren't that bad."

"Chips and salsa, def," she says. "And maybe a veggie burrito. I don't trust the meat here."

"Sounds good," I say.

The waitress appears at our table a second later. It's Kalia Spinelli, who I may or may not have hooked up with last year. "Oh," she says when she sees me. "It's you." She says it like she's surprised to see me. Which I guess she probably is, since I never called her after we hooked up.

"Oh, hi, Kalia," I say politely. "It's nice to see you."

"Yeah, well, it's not nice to see you," she says. She poises her hand over her pad and sighs. But she doesn't ask to take our order or anything.

"Um, I'm going to have a virgin piña colada," I say.

146

She purses her lips and then makes this big show of writing it down, like it's a huge imposition. Her pen is pushing so hard into the paper that I'm afraid she's going to push it right though and into her hand.

"And what would you like to drink, Harper?" I ask.

"I'll have the same," she says.

But Kalia doesn't write it down. Instead she just flips her pen over and taps it against her pad. "Who are you?" she asks.

"Me?" Harper looks confused.

"Yeah."

"I'm Harper."

Kalia purses her lips and looks at Harper, like she's thinking about this. "Well, Harper, I'd be careful if I were you." She points at me. "This one's kind of an asshole." And then she turns around and walks away.

I sit there for a moment, stunned. Obviously I've had girls be upset with me before. But usually I'm able to talk my way out of it, and if I'm not, it's not a big deal. I mean, if a girl says something rude to me, it usually doesn't matter. I've never had a girl confront me about being an asshole right in front of a girl I wanted to impress. Actually, I've never really wanted to impress a girl before, so I guess it makes sense.

I give Harper a smile. "So," I say, "are you definitely set on what you want to eat?"

"Who was that?"

"Kalia Spinelli," I say. "She's in our grade."

"Yeah, I know."

"Oh." Then why did she ask?

"I mean, I know who she is. I'm just wondering who she is, you know, to you." She fiddles with one of the paper menus, folding the corner back into an accordion shape.

"I used to hang out with her," I say carefully.

"How?"

"How?"

"Yeah, how did you guys hang out? Like, in what way?"

"You know, like, uh . . ." If I'm being honest, I don't totally remember. I know that makes me sound like a total asshole, but the details are hazy. "We hooked up," I try.

"And then you did something to make her mad."

It's a statement, not a question. "Yes."

"Like blew her off?"

I shrug.

"You don't remember? Or you don't want to tell me?"

I sigh. "Look, can we talk about something else?"

"Sure." But she doesn't sound like she means it.

Kalia comes back and slams down the drinks we ordered. Piña colada sloshes over to the side of my cup and splashes onto my wrist. Kalia gives me a satisfied look, and I quickly pick up my drink and move it farther away from her, just in case she gets any ideas about picking it up and throwing it in my face. "My boss says I have to wait on you, even though I think you're a total douche," she reports.

"Oh," I say, wiping up the spilled drink. "How lucky for me. We're going to have some nachos and two veggie burritos." I was going to have a chicken burrito, but the food here is sketchy on a good day, never mind when some girl who is looking for revenge is going to be serving it. Who knows what kind of crazy things she's going to end up doing to my meal. Come to think of it, I probably shouldn't even be ordering anything.

"Okay," Kalia says. Then she turns to Harper. "You should make him pay the check. You're going to need the money for your therapy bill."

"Wow," I say once Kalia disappears. I roll my eyes. "What a drama queen."

"I guess." Harper twists her hands in her lap and looks around the restaurant hesitantly. There are tons of people here from school, and her eyes flick over all of them. I wonder if she's trying to figure out which girls I've messed around with. I want to reassure her, but I'm not exactly sure what to say.

"Hey—" I start. But before I can finish, Jackson Burr saunters up to our table.

"So listen," he says, and grabs a bar stool from a four-top near us. He pulls it over to our table and sits down, like he and I are in the middle of a conversation and not two people who hate each other. "It was weird the other night, right? At the batting cages? Anyway, I've been thinking, and I've decided we should talk about it."

I feel a rage start to burn inside me. First because Jackson's here, and second because he's bringing up things that are ridiculously personal and he's bringing them up in front of Harper. I don't want to talk about what happened at the batting cages.

"Jackson," I say, trying to force my voice to stay upbeat. "You know better than to crash one of my dates."

He looks over at Harper, like he's seeing her for the first time. "This is a date?" he asks skeptically.

"Yes," I say firmly. I know I wasn't sure I wanted to be making that declaration, but now that I'm saying it, it feels right.

"Okay." Jackson looks at Harper again, his eyes lingering on her body for a second longer than necessary, the same way they did that night at the batting cages. *Don't do that*, a voice inside me screams. *She's mine.* I'm shocked by the ferocity of it. "We met at the batting cages the other night, right?"

Harper nods and then takes a sip of her drink.

Jackson smiles and then partially pulls a flask out of the front pocket of his long-sleeved T-shirt. He motions to Harper. "You want to make it a real one?"

"No, she doesn't," I say. "Jesus, Jackson." What the hell is wrong with him, bringing alcohol here? This isn't some seedy bar where you can get away with that kind of thing.

"What?" he asks. "Like you don't want some?"

"I don't." I turn away from him.

"Right, so it's like that now?" Jackson laughs bitterly as he puts the flask away.

Harper's looking at me curiously from across the table. Shit. She's probably going to get all worried now and start freaking out about me having some kind of drinking problem. Which I don't. Just because I used to get drunk with the team now and then doesn't mean I have a problem. And after I fucked up my shoulder, yeah, I took the edge off with a little alcohol, but who wouldn't have?

I haven't had a drink since then.

"It's not like anything," I say. Then I get quiet.

"Whatever," Jackson says, running his fingers through his hair and sighing. "Look, we need to talk."

"No, we don't."

"Yeah, we do. Come on. Come sit with us." He motions over to the corner, where a bunch of guys from the team—Dan Martin, Brody Lansing, and Sawyer French—are sitting at a high-top. There are girls over there, laughing and flirting and jostling for position so they can sit next to whoever it is they've decided they want to go home with. If this were a few months ago, I'd be over there with them, feeling sloppy from the booze, my eyes halfway closed as I tried to figure out which girl I was going to kiss later that night. My muscles would be aching from practice, but it would be a good ache, the kind of ache that makes you feel like you're alive.

"I told you, I'm on a date."

Jackson stands up and shakes his head. "She can come too." He picks up our drinks and then motions to Kalia to let her know that Harper and I are going to be moving to his table.

"No," I say, "we don't want to go."

"It's okay," Harper says. "I don't mind sitting over there."

I can tell she's just saying it because she thinks I want to. Of course she minds going over there to sit with those assholes.

"No, it's okay," I tell her. "We're staying right here."

"See?" Jackson says. "She said it's okay. Come on." He starts to walk away with our drinks, and suddenly, before I can stop myself, I'm out of my chair and grabbing at the back of his shirt. I'm only trying to stop him from moving, but my grip must be tighter than I planned, because it causes Jackson to spin around. A bunch of piña colada sloshes out of the glasses and oozes over his fingers onto the floor.

"What the fuck, Mattingly?" he curses. "What the hell is your problem?"

"My problem," I say, "is that you can't mind your own damn business." I take the dripping glasses out of his hands.

"I'm supposed to mind my own business?" Jackson repeats incredulously. He moves closer to me so that he's in my face now, and I can smell the alcohol on him. "You totally just drop out, no goodbye, nothing, and I'm supposed to mind my own damn business? That's all I've been doing, Penn! And I'm fucking sick of this shit."

"Oh, right," I mutter. "You're such a victim. None of this is because of you, right, Jackson?"

"What's that supposed to mean?" Jackson asks. And then his voice softens just a little. "Penn—" he starts, but before he can say anything, something snaps inside me.

It's like a switch or the break of a branch. That's how fast it overtakes me. I turn and haul one of the piña coladas at the wall as hard as I can. The glass immediately shatters, and sticky liquid oozes everywhere. A searing pain shoots through my bad shoulder. But I can hardly even feel it.

"Penn!" Harper cries. She stands up, her eyes wide. "Penn, please, what are you doing?"

"Jesus Christ, man," Jackson says, shaking his head as he looks down at the broken glass and spilled drink. "You are even more fucked up than I thought."

"Penn," Harper says, pulling on my sleeve. "Penn, come on. Let's get out of here."

From across the room I can see Kalia whispering to some douchey-looking guy in a button-up shirt who looks like the manager. He starts to walk over to us, probably so he can kick me out.

But I'm not going to give him a chance.

I turn around and walk out.

It's not until I'm halfway to my car that I realize Harper is following me.

Harper

Whoa.

Okay.

I will not freak out, I will not freak out, I will not freak out.

I just need to keep cool. Yes, that was crazy intense. Yes, it was crazy scary. Yes, Penn broke a glass and basically got us kicked out of the restaurant. But I can't get all worked up about it, because that's not going to help the situation.

Thank God he didn't hurt anyone. For a second I was pretty sure he was going to throw that drink right at Jackson's face, or maybe even punch him. That's how mad Penn looked. I could see it building inside him until finally he just snapped.

I follow him out to the parking lot, and he's all broody and dark.

"Hey," I say, running to catch up. "What was that about?"

His shoulders are hunched over, and his hands are in his pockets and he's walking so fast, I can hardly keep pace. "Nothing."

"Well, obviously it was *something*," I say. "I mean, you don't just go throwing glasses at walls unless there's something going on."

We're at his truck now, and he reaches into his pocket and pulls out his keys. His hands are shaking a little.

"Penn," I say, reaching out and putting my hand on his. "Seriously, what the hell is going on?"

"I told you, nothing." He unlocks the door and then goes to get inside.

But I just stand there. No way I'm getting into a car with him when he's all worked up like this. How do I know he's in any condition to drive?

"You coming?" he asks.

"No." I shake my head. "I'm not getting into a car with you until you tell me what the hell is going on."

He looks at me, his eyes blazing, his breathing heavy. My pulse is racing, the anticipation of what's going to happen hanging in the air. Is he going to tell me what's going on? Or is he going to try to make me get into the car with him without telling me anything? If he does, I won't. I'll call Anna and have her come pick me up. Or even better, I'll call my mom and have her come pick me up. She would love that. She's always talking about how if I ever get stranded at some party or something and there's no one sober to drive me home that I should call her and she'll come get me, no questions asked. It'll be like a bonding moment.

"Harper," Penn says, "get into the car."

"No." I stand my ground. "Not until you explain."

"Harper," he says again. "I don't want to have to leave you here, but I will."

I laugh. "Really?" I say. "Really? That's what you have to say for yourself? You don't want to have to leave me here, but you will?" I shake my head. I am so done with this. "Whatever, Penn. Just go. You're good at leaving me places anyway."

I turn around, and as soon as I do, my throat squeezes and tears burn in my eyes. I'm mad at him, but I'm mad at myself too, for trusting him. He's an asshole. That's what my instincts were telling me, and somehow I let myself get all wrapped up in him.

I must be crazy.

I take a few steps back toward the restaurant, fumbling in my purse for my phone. And then he's there.

Behind me, his footsteps matching mine.

He doesn't say anything—he just keeps walking with me.

Our footsteps fall into a matching rhythm, but he still doesn't talk.

I finish pulling out my phone.

"Who are you calling?" he asks finally.

"My mom," I say.

"Your mom?" He seems shocked and appalled.

"Yeah." I'm struggling to keep my voice from shaking. The last thing I want is for him to know I was about to cry. "I'm going to have her come pick me up."

I start dialing, but he reaches out and pulls the phone out of my hands gently. "Harper," he whispers. He's looking at me with this intense look on his face, halfway between sadness and longing, and it's so angsty and wanty that I think I'm in some kind of romance novel.

"No," I say. "Don't look at me like that. You don't get to look at me like that."

He's still holding my phone. He reaches out and pulls me close to him, and then, suddenly, his lips are on mine. This time his kiss is different than it was the other night. The other night it was flirty and fun, with darkness just below the surface. This time the danger is right there, in the kiss, showing itself in the way his lips move against mine, the way his arms encircle my waist and pull me so close to him that I can feel the hardness of his chest.

I lose myself in the kiss, letting him take over, letting myself melt against his body. I'm not thinking about what just happened back in the restaurant, I'm not thinking about the fact that he just tried to ditch me for the second time today, or what it means that every girl we come into contact with he has some kind of history with.

Instead, all I'm thinking about is how good this feels. His hands are around my waist, holding me tight, and then finally he pulls away.

"Harper," he whispers again. The way he says my name fills my body with heat. No one has ever said my name like that before. "Come on," he says. "Let's get out of here."

My heart is racing and my body is all flushed. A breeze moves through the parking lot, pushing my hair back from my face, and even though the air is hot, it feels cool and good against my skin.

"No," I say. "I'm not . . . I can't . . ." I take a deep breath and try to clear my thoughts. "You can't just kiss me or leave me anytime something comes up. Don't you . . . I mean, why can't we talk about this?"

He gets a pained look on his face. Then finally he nods. "Okay," he says. "Fine."

But he doesn't move. "Okay fine, what?"

"Okay, fine, let's talk."

"Okay."

"Okay."

We're still standing close, and I can feel his body heat through the thin T-shirt I'm wearing. I take a step back.

"Go ahead, talk," he says.

"Tell me about Jackson."

"That asshole? There's nothing to—"

"Penn."

He sighs. "Fine. Then can we at least go somewhere else?"

"Like where?"

He shrugs. "I don't know. You pick."

"My house." I didn't know I wanted him to come over until I'm saying the words. But it makes sense. I want him on my turf. Everything about our relationship has been on his terms up until this point, and now I want some of the power.

"Your house?"

"Why not?"

"I don't know, because . . ."

"My house," I say. "Take it or leave it."

He hesitates, and for one horrible moment I think he's going to say no. Then finally his face softens. "Take it."

By the time we get to my house, I have five text messages from Anna, all of them asking me about what happened at the Sailing Burrito. Which is crazy, because Anna wasn't even *at* the Sailing Burrito.

Which means she must have found out about the Penn-Jackson incident from someone texting her or Facebooking about it. I try telling her that we'll talk about it later, but she's insistent. She keeps texting, and when I don't reply, she starts calling. I send all her calls to voicemail—I can't deal with her right now. I know she wants gossip, and she's also probably worried about me, but for now she's going to have to settle for just knowing that I'm okay. She's not going to die if she has to wait an hour to talk to me.

When we pull up in front of my house, the light is on in my mom's room. On the way here I called and asked if Penn could come over. My mom said he could but that I'm not allowed to have him in my room. Still, my mom is upstairs, apparently willing to give us our space.

"Is your mom going to give me the third degree again?"

Penn asks as we walk up the sidewalk and I open the front door.

I shake my head. "No," I say. "But I probably will."

He follows me into the kitchen, and I have to admit, it's a little bit strange. I thought that having Penn here, where I'm comfortable, would make me feel . . . I don't know, more secure or something. But instead it just feels awkward.

Plus I just realized that if Penn wants to leave, he can simply walk out. At least if we were out somewhere, he'd have to take me home first. I know I shouldn't care about that. If he's the kind of guy who's going to have mood swings so severe that he would walk out of my house never to be heard from again, then I should just write him off.

But I can't. I hate the fact that even though he's here, standing in my kitchen with me, everything seems so fragile. I'm always afraid I'm never going to see him again, or I'm going to say something that's going to scare him away.

"Do you want something to drink?" I ask. The house is quiet. The fact that my mom didn't come downstairs to say hello as soon as we got here makes me certain she's not going to.

He shrugs. "I guess."

I open the refrigerator. "Um, we have soda, water, orange juice . . ."

He moves behind me, then stoops down and looks over my shoulder. "You got any chocolate milk?"

"Chocolate milk?"

"Yeah. You know, milk mixed with chocolate?"

"What are you, ten?"

He looks at me and sighs. "Chocolate milk is an excellent drink. It's good for muscle recovery, and it also tastes delicious."

"Well, I don't have any. You'll have to settle for something else."

He nods, accepting it. "Orange juice."

I pull the carton out and pour two glasses, then hand him one. He takes a sip, and so do I. Then we just sort of stand there, looking at each other. This is probably the part where I'm supposed to ask him if he wants to watch a movie or something, but I'm afraid if we get wrapped up in doing something else, we're not going to get to talk. And that was the whole point of coming here.

"So, what do you want to do?" he asks. The heaviness that was surrounding him earlier is gone, and now he's grinning at me. "Wanna watch a movie or something?"

"No." I shake my head firmly. "We were going to talk, remember?"

"We can talk while we watch a movie." He takes another step toward me, but I take a step back. If he kisses me again, I'm not sure I'm going to have the strength to stop him. And who knows what's going to happen then? It's not like he could just ravish my body or anything—we can't go into my room, and besides, my mom is right upstairs. But still. There's a perfectly good couch in the living room. A flash of us on that couch making out enters my mind, and I push it out and take another step away from him.

"Come on," I say. "Let's go outside."

I take him out back to our deck, then sit down across from him near the fire pit.

"Can we have a fire?" he asks.

I nod, then reach under and turn on the propane. I pick up the lighter that's sitting on the side of the pit and light the fire. The flames burn and dance, turning different shades of red, yellow, orange, and blue. I curl my legs up under me and sip my juice. "So," I say. "Let's talk."

"Okay." He shrugs, like talking isn't a big deal, like he hasn't been completely shut down since I met him.

"Okay." I take a deep breath. "So why'd you get so mad at Jackson tonight?"

"Because Jackson's an asshole."

"A little more, please?"

He sighs and then leans over and looks into the fire. "Jackson is . . . he's from a part of my life that I don't really want to revisit."

"What part?"

"You know, the part from before."

"Before you hurt your shoulder?"

I see the pain flash through his eyes for a moment, bright and searing, and then it's gone, pushed back to wherever he keeps it hidden. "Yeah."

"But why?"

"Why is he from that part of my life?"

"No, why does there have to be a before and after?"

"I don't know." He shrugs. "There just does. And Jackson's from before. So now I need to start making new memories." He gives me that sexy little grin of his and then scoots his chair over so it's right up against mine. He pulls my legs up and drapes them over his lap.

I lean back and look at him. "You're really frustrating, you know that?"

"How so?"

"You won't tell me anything!"

"I just told you what you wanted to know." He slides one of my flip-flops off, and it clatters onto the deck. Then he starts rubbing my ankle. His touch sends sparks all up and down my body.

"No, you didn't. You talked around it."

He sighs and doesn't say anything for a second. He looks back at the fire, and the colors of the flame swirl in his dark eyes. His hand is still rubbing my skin. "It's complicated," he says. "Baseball is . . . Baseball *was* my life. It defined me. So when I couldn't play anymore, all of that stuff had to go away."

"Including Jackson."

"Including Jackson."

"Why?"

"Because being around him was too hard, I guess." He shakes his head, seemingly confused. "Wow, I've never said that out loud before."

"Not even to him?" I'm shocked. I can't imagine just getting rid of Anna and not at least giving her some kind of explanation. I always thought Jackson was just being a dick, but if my best friend blew me off with no explanation, I'd probably be pretty pissed too.

"Nope."

"Wow." I shake my head. "No wonder you guys almost got into a fight tonight."

"What do you mean?"

"Well, you just stopped talking to him. He's obviously angry. And holding it in must be extremely frustrating for you. All those feelings are just sitting inside you, building up with nowhere to go."

"I don't have anything building up inside me," he says.

He doesn't sound defensive, though. Instead he sounds kind of sad. I sit up in my chair and move closer to him so that our knees are touching. He reaches out and takes my hand, his thumb moving in little circles against my palm.

"Penn," I say. "I'm . . ." I want to say that I'm really sorry, but I don't think that's going to go over so well. I don't think he wants anyone to feel sorry for him. And the thing is, I *don't* really feel sorry for him. I just feel sad that he feels he needs to keep everything inside.

"You don't have to say you're sorry," he says. "It's a shitty situation, but it's not your fault."

"What happened?" I ask softly. "You know, to your shoulder?"

This time, he turns and looks at me when he talks. "I tore it," he says. "It's . . . it's kind of shredded."

"And there's nothing you can do? No surgery or anything? No other doctor you can try?"

He opens his mouth to say something, but then changes his mind. He shakes his head. The pain in his eyes is so over-whelming that in that moment all I want to do is take it away. So I move toward him, my finger reaching out and tracing the hard line of his jaw. There's a little bit of stubble on his cheeks, but other than that his skin is smooth and soft. His lips are so tempting that it's only a second before I can't take it anymore. I lean over and kiss him softly.

He shifts himself over, so that we're both on the same chair, and we fall back onto the chaise, our legs tangling as our kiss deepens. His hands move down my sides, and I feel dizzy and light-headed, almost like I'm about to lose control of my own body. He tastes like peppermint and orange juice, and it's a heady combination, one that's making me realize what people are talking about when they say they're losing themselves in someone.

I'm losing myself in Penn.

We kiss and kiss and kiss and kiss, and this time I don't try to resist it.

Penn

I didn't tell her.

About Dr. Marzetti.

Harper asked me, point-blank, if there was any chance my shoulder could be fixed, if there was any chance I could get a surgery, or a new doctor, or *something*. The sad thing is, she's the only one who's ever asked me that.

Even my dad, the day the doctor at Mass General looked at my X-rays and said there was no way I was going to ever play again, never asked if we should get a second opinion. Instead he disappeared for eight days. When he came back, we didn't bring it up, unless it was him taking little jabs at me about how I had lost my chance at a scholarship, or to let me know that he thought it was ridiculous for me to be spending time at the batting cages.

But I didn't tell Harper about Dr. Marzetti. I was going to, I was about to, I was saying things out loud that I'd never said out loud to anyone, things I hadn't even really admitted to myself, but I couldn't tell her about Dr. Marzetti.

First, it's such a long shot that it's not really worth talking about. I don't even have an appointment with her, and it doesn't look like I'm ever going to be able to get one. Second, if I did tell Harper, she would definitely start asking me about it. And I'm not sure I can take that. I don't want to have to worry about her bothering me about what's going on, or if I've heard anything, or what the chances are that I'm going to get an appointment. Most of the time I just want to forget about baseball. And if I give Harper an invitation to ask me about my shoulder, she can bring it up anytime she wants, forcing me to have to deal with it.

And that's something I definitely do not want.

For a second I was afraid she was going to push it, but she didn't.

Instead she kissed me.

And I kissed her back, and it was the best kiss I ever had in my life. It was weird—the kiss was great, but it's what was behind it that made it amazing. There was emotion. We kissed for what seemed like forever. With any other girl I'd have pushed for more. I would have wanted more. But with Harper, just kissing was enough.

I had to leave at midnight when her mom called out the window and told us it was probably time for me to go, since it was a school night. Luckily she didn't come downstairs, since we were pretty disheveled at that point.

When I left Harper's house, it was hard to tear myself away. I wanted to stay with her, wanted to hold her close and never let her out of my sight. She walked me to the door, and I kissed her goodbye. Her lips were swollen and bee-stung from everything we'd done, and her hair was all tangled in this sexy way that was driving me crazy.

When I got into my car and started driving home, I immediately missed her.

With Harper everything was different.

So different.

Everything just felt completely *right*.

Being at her house.

Her mom calling downstairs and telling us it was midnight and that I had to go home. All of it was so normal, it just felt . . . I don't know, natural.

When I get back to my house, no one else is awake. I climb into bed, and for a while I can't fall asleep. All I can think about is her—the way she tastes, the way she feels, the emotions she stirs up inside me. But when I finally do fall asleep, my sleep is sound and restful.

When I wake up the next morning, the house is quiet. I'm not sure where everyone is, and I don't care. All I can think about is getting to school and seeing Harper. I think about sending her a text and seeing if she needs a ride, but then I have this moment of uncertainty. What if Harper isn't as into what happened last night as I am? What if she thinks I'm crazy for what I did at the Sailing Burrito, and so she decided that, make-out session or not, it's best to stay away from me?

The thought is kind of shocking. I've never had to worry about a girl not being into me. It just doesn't happen. And if it did, I wouldn't even ever know about it, because by the time they'd start to have doubts, I'd be on to the next girl.

When I pull into the student parking lot, all I can think about is finding Harper, and I wonder if maybe I should send her a text to find out where she is.

But then I spot her, over on the lawn, sitting with a couple of her friends.

She's wearing this adorable little yellow summer dress. I've never seen her in a dress before. As she leans over, the bottom of the fabric rises up, giving me a view of her legs. Jesus Christ. What was I thinking, just kissing her last night? I walk over, not sure exactly how this is going to go.

One of the friends she's with is Anna. But the boy, I don't think I know him. Nick or something?

As I get closer, Harper looks up and smiles.

And in that moment I know it's going to be okay.

"Hey," she says, standing up and walking toward me. She takes my hand. "Come and meet my friends."

Anna and the boy look up from where they're sitting in the grass. Their heads are bowed down, and it looks like maybe they're looking at sheet music.

"This is Nico," Harper says.

"Hey," Nico says. He gives me the head nod that guys give each other.

"Hey."

"And you know Anna," Harper says. She points at Anna, who looks up at me and narrows her eyes suspiciously.

I'm used to the friends of girls I've hooked up with not liking me. What I'm not used to is caring.

"Hey, Anna," I say, giving her a friendly smile. "Nice to see you again."

She purses her lips. "Hello, Penn," she says. "You're looking very relaxed for someone who's the talk of the school."

"I'm the talk of the school?" I ask. "Why?" Is it possible that everyone already knows about me and Harper? Just from one night out at the Sailing Burrito?

"Well, when you throw a glass at a wall in front of everyone, people think it's kind of a big deal," Anna says, all snotty like.

"Oh," I say. "That."

"Yeah," Anna says. "That."

"Anna," Harper says warningly. She turns to me. "It's not a big deal, Penn. You know people. They just like to talk about stuff."

"Yeah, stuff that's crazy," Anna says. "Stuff that insane people do."

I swallow. "I got angry," I say, shrugging. "It happens." Now I'm starting to get a little annoyed. Why should I have to explain myself to this girl? She doesn't even know me.

"Not to me," Anna says. "If I got angry, there's no way I would throw a glass across the room." She leans back on her hands, locking her elbows behind her. "People are saying that you were this close to throwing it at Jackson."

"That's ridiculous," I say, rolling my eyes. "I wasn't going to throw it at Jackson."

"That's good," Anna says. "Because if you were, that would indicate you have a serious anger problem."

"Relax, Anna," Nico says. "You don't understand, because you're not a guy."

Anna looks shocked by this, like Nico has just declared that a woman can't be president or something. "What's that supposed to mean?"

"It just means that girls are different. You all talk behind each other's backs and gossip about each other. Sometimes men just need to get it out. The old-fashioned way."

"By punching each other?" Anna says incredulously.

Nico shrugs. "If that's what it comes to."

Anna's mouth drops. "I cannot believe you're taking his side."

"I'm not taking anyone's side," Nico says. "I'm just stating facts."

Anna's face is turning red, and I'm wondering why she's getting so worked up. I mean, I get that she and Harper are like OMG BFF or whatever it is the girls are calling it these days, but come on. Can she really be that upset with me? She hasn't even given me a chance.

But then I catch her looking at Nico, and I get it. She has

a thing for him. She has a thing for Nico, and so yeah, she's annoyed with me because she thinks I'm not good enough for Harper, but now she's getting doubly annoyed with me because she thinks that Nico is siding with me instead of her.

Jesus, this is getting into, like, soap opera shit.

"You never take my side," Anna says. She starts to pack up the sheet music that's sitting in front of her, shoving it into a folder angrily.

"What are you talking about?" Nico asks. He sounds perplexed in the way that guys do after girls say something that makes no sense whatsoever. "I always take your side."

"Not today!" she fumes. "Where is my music for *Wicked*?" she demands. "I just had it!"

"I saw *Wicked* in New York a couple of years ago," I offer. "I took my mom for her birthday." I don't mention that it was a family trip, and that my dad left at intermission to go to the bathroom and then didn't come back until after the show, completely shitfaced, and then he and Braden got into a fight, and so Braden and I ended up wandering around Times Square at night like a couple of vagrants because we had no money and couldn't stand to be around my parents. That was before Braden discovered the wonderful allures of marijuana.

"You went to *Wicked*?" Anna asks. "That figures."

I frown. "Why does that figure?" *Wicked* is very girly. It would make no sense for me to be at that show. I should have been at something a little more manly, like a comedy show, or maybe that Spiderman show everyone was so worked up about because the actors kept getting hurt. That I went to *Wicked* shows that I'm actually very in touch with my soft side.

"Because *Wicked* is the show people go to when they want to make themselves feel all cultured. But in reality they have no idea that *Wicked* is overproduced fluff."

I shrug. "My mom picked it." If Anna doesn't like *Wicked*, why does she have the music for it?

"Yeah, well, people like your mom have no taste."

"Anna!" Harper exclaims.

But I don't really care that Anna said that. She's right. My mom doesn't have that much taste.

"No, it's okay," I say. "But why do you have music from *Wicked* if you hate it so much?"

Anna sighs. "You wouldn't get it."

"Anna's trying to get into Juilliard," Harper explains. "And she needs to do an audition piece."

"And one of the songs from *Wicked* has been assigned to me," Anna says. "So I have to learn it."

"Oh," I say. "That sounds fun."

"It's not *fun*," she says. "It's extremely stressful and overwhelming."

I nod. It doesn't make any sense, but I'm not even mad that she's being a bitch to me. It's like I'm excited for the challenge of winning her over. She doesn't know me, so it's not like she can really hate me *that* much. I'll just have to show her the real me.

But obviously connecting with her over this whole Juilliard thing is a bad idea. Not only is the world of music foreign to me, but I just can't relate to the college admissions process. Once I got hurt, I completely forgot about college. I've hardly even thought about it. It's probably something I *should* think about—I mean, what am I going to do after graduation? Get a job? I guess I'm going to have to.

Suddenly I'm depressed. What's the point of even graduating? I'm probably going to end up at some shitty job making shitty money. Harper's going to Ballard. It's in Rhode Island, just far enough away for her to meet some other guy.

I force myself to focus back on the conversation. But no one's saying anything. We're all just sort of standing there with tension in the air.

There's tension between me and Anna, tension between Anna and Nico. There's even a little bit of tension between me and Harper.

And that's when the school nurse decides to descend on our little group.

I'm very familiar with the school nurse, because back in the day I'd fake a lot of illnesses. I'd go down to the nurse's office clutching my stomach and pretending I'd just thrown up in the bathroom. They have to let you go home if you've thrown up. It's, like, a rule or something. And since no one could prove I hadn't, they'd have to let me go.

It wasn't even that big a deal. The nurse didn't really care that I was lying. She's actually kind of cool, in an old, doddering-woman kind of way.

"Penn!" she exclaims when she sees me. "I haven't seen you

in a while!" She sounds like I'm an old friend she's missed, and not just a delinquent student who misused her trust to get out of going to class.

"Yeah, well," I say, shrugging. "I've gotten my stomach issues worked out."

"Yeah, I'll bet." She purses her lips and looks at me knowingly. "Anyway, I'm looking for a student, and I'm hoping you can help." She waves a list of names in front of me. "These students are trying to get out of getting their physicals, so I'm trying to track them down."

Next to me I feel Harper stiffen.

The nurse glances down at the paper. "Do any of you know Harper Fairbanks?"

Nico averts his gaze and stares down at the paper in front of him. Anna lets out this big sigh, like she can't believe the jig is up.

And then, before I even know what's happening, I say to the nurse with a straight face, "No. I don't know Harper Fairbanks." I add in a little shrug for good measure.

"It's the strangest thing," the nurse says, shaking her head. "I swear, I cannot find this girl. I've tried everything, and I just cannot find her." The nurse seems flummoxed, which is a nod to Harper's stealth avoidance skills, obviously.

"I think she moved away," Anna says. "Didn't she move away, Nico?"

Nico frowns. "Harper Fairbanks? Yeah, I think she might have moved away. She used to be in my science class, but then I think she moved to Florida. She had allergies or something, so her parents moved her right out." He makes a miming motion, like her parents physically picked her up and set her down in Florida.

"Yup," I agree. "Right out."

"Because of allergies?" The nurse seems shocked. "I didn't know allergies in New England could get that bad."

"Well, it wasn't *air* allergies," I say at the same time that Anna says, "Well, she had a condition."

"It was, um, food allergies," I say. "A condition of food allergies. Like, really bad ones."

"But why did she have to go to Florida?" the nurse persists. What is she, some kind of crime-scene investigator or something?

"Um, well, she was getting all these hives," I say.

"From clams," Nico says.

"Yes!" Anna's all over it. "Clams! And since there's so much clam chowder in New England, she just had to go."

"It was very serious," I say. "She might have died if she even got in contact with a clam. Or anything that, you know, lived in a shell."

"Yeah," Harper says, apparently feeling confident enough to start chiming in on her own imaginary fate. "It's like those kids who can't be around peanuts."

"Huh," the nurse says. "I've never heard of anything like that. Well, thanks anyway." She shakes her head and walks away, mumbling about food additives.

Once she's out of earshot, the four of us look at each other and then immediately start laughing.

"Oh my God," Harper says. "That was epic."

"I seriously thought you were busted." Nico shakes his head. "Food allergies? Jesus, I can't believe she bought that."

"Good one, Penn," Anna says. She gives me a grudging smile.

"Thanks," I say.

Harper beams at me.

I reach out and take her hand. Her fingers wrap around mine, and I've never felt anything better.

Harper

Okay, so that was pretty awesome. Not only did Penn completely and totally win Anna over, but he was somehow able to save me from the school nurse. (And seriously, when did the school nurse become such a stalker? I mean, I understand she's just doing her job, but really? Coming outside and asking people if they know me? That's kind of taking things to a whole other level. That's, like, restraining-order territory.)

Once Anna and Nico head to first period, Penn leans me up against the side of the school and kisses me. It makes my heart pound just as fast as it did last night. Everything about him is exciting. Last night it was exciting because he was finally letting me in. This morning it's exciting because he's kissing me right here at school, out in the open where anyone can see.

"I missed you," he breathes into my hair.

"I missed you, too," I say back.

But it turns out I don't have to miss him.

Because we're together after that, every moment pretty much, for the next three weeks. At school we meet between classes and do our homework together at lunch, stealing kisses in between math problems. After school Penn will drop me off at the dance studio, then head to Whole Foods, where he buys snacks. Then he keeps me company in the office while we eat whatever delicious treats he's picked up that day. When I'm done with work, sometimes Penn goes home, but usually he'll come back to my house. We sit out by the fire pit and eat s'mores and then make out after my mom goes to sleep. Weekends are reserved for our real "dates"—we'll go to dinner, see a movie, or take long walks. One Saturday we go to the beach, staying there all day until our skin is sunburned and our shoes are filled with sand.

Everything is going great until Anna starts to freak out.

She shows up at my house on a Friday morning before school. Her hair is disheveled, her face is flushed, and her eyes are wide. She's holding a cup of Starbucks coffee in each hand.

"We need to talk," she says.

"What's wrong?" I ask. "Is it your mom?" Anna's mom had breast cancer a few years ago. She's totally fine now, and in remission, but there's always a chance that the cancer could come back.

"What? No, my mom's fine." She shakes her head.

"Okay." I walk out of my house, then turn around and lock the door.

"Ride with me to school?" Anna asks.

"Sure." Lately I've been riding to school with Penn, so I pull my phone out and text him to let him know that Anna's going to take me today.

"So something happened last night," she says once we get into her car.

"What kind of something?"

"The kind of something that . . . I don't know, the kind of something that's making my head all confused."

"It's making my head confused too," I say. My phone beeps with a text.

Penn.

C u at school beautiful.

My heart flutters in my chest. He's called me beautiful before, but I'm still not used to it. How can you really get used to something like that? A hot guy calling you beautiful when you've never thought of yourself that way? Not that I have low self-esteem or anything. But I've always thought of myself as kind of average. Or maybe a little bit—

"Hello!" Anna says. "Can you focus on me for once?"

"For once? What's that supposed to mean?"

"It means that I have something to talk about, and all you can think about is texting with Penn." We're at a stoplight, and she reaches down and pulls her coffee out of the cup holder and takes a sip. She's obviously pissed off at me, though, because she does it all herky-jerky and some of the coffee spills out of the top of the cup and onto her hand.

"That's not all I can think about." I reach into the glove compartment and pull out a napkin.

I hand it to her, and she wipes at the coffee angrily, then balls up the napkin and throws it into the backseat. "Yeah, it is," she says. "You've been spending every single second with him lately."

"Whoa." I shake my head. "We need to start over. If you want to talk about me and Penn, that's one thing. But you showed up at my house this morning saying something weird happened."

She doesn't say anything for a second, just reaches over and rolls down her window. Her hair blows softly in the breeze. "Okay," she says. "I'm sorry. You're right. I'm just freaking out right now, and I'm probably looking for someone to take it out on."

"Okay," I say, shrugging and deciding to let it go. Anna doesn't usually snap at me, and I can see how she might be a little annoyed that I've been spending all my free time with Penn. "But, Anna, what are you freaking out about?"

"Well, last night . . . I'm not sure exactly what happened, but basically . . . I mean . . ." She licks her lips. "Nico and I kissed."

"What?!" I scream so loud that Anna winces.

"Shhh!" she says. "Jesus, Harper, you're going to blow out my eardrums."

"Wait, you guys *kissed*?"

"No. I mean, yes. I mean, sort of. I don't know! It was weird."

"Tell me every detail." I cannot believe she didn't call me last night. Not that we've really been talking much on the phone lately. But still. She could have at least texted me.

"Okay, so we were at my house, and I was running through my music for my audition. He was listening to me practice, you know, like he usually does. And it was just horrible, Harper. Completely horrible."

"Him listening?"

"No." She shakes her head again. "My singing."

"Okay." I know better than to refute this point. Anna goes through these phases where she gets all emotional about her music and insists she sounds like crap. If you tell her she sounds great (which she does), she yells and says that you don't know what you're talking about, that you don't have an ear for music. Which is actually true in my case. I'm completely tone deaf. Every time I try to watch those singing reality shows, I always think someone sounds great, and the next thing I know the judges are talking about how awful the person sounds.

"Anyway, I started freaking out about it, because my audition is this weekend, and I really need to make sure I'm on point. So Nico was trying to console me, and then he gave me a hug."

"And then?" God, this is torture. It's like trying to pull teeth with her. Why doesn't she just spit it out?

"And then he started stroking my hair. And then he kissed me."

"Oh my God!" I screech. "Anna, this is huge! Was it good?"

"The kiss?"

"Yes, the kiss!"

"Well, it wasn't the kind of kiss that could be considered good or bad." We're pulling into the school parking lot now, and she guides her car into our parking spot.

"What do you mean?" I unbuckle my seat belt and start pawing through my bag. I left in such a rush this morning that I'm not sure if I remembered my math homework.

"It was on my head," Anna says. She turns the car off. I look over at her, and she's staring out the windshield toward school.

I frown. "What do you mean?"

"I mean that he kissed me on my head."

"Oh." I try to keep the deflation I'm feeling out of my voice. He kissed her on the head? That doesn't sound like it's that good a story. I was picturing it more like she was crying and he started to, like, kiss her tears away, and then before she knew what was happening, his mouth was on hers and they had to tear themselves away from each other before they had sex and ruined their whole friendship.

But kissing her on the head? That definitely sounds kind of lame. Then again, what do I know? Up until recently my experience with kissing was zero. Maybe Nico wanted to kiss Anna on the mouth but she panicked and turned her head, and so he had no choice but to kiss her forehead. And now she's freaking out because she really *did* want to kiss him and she thinks she missed her chance.

"Well," I say slowly. "Maybe he wanted to kiss your mouth, but you turned your head."

"I didn't turn my head."

"Oh."

We sit there for a second, both thinking about this. Her car is making this sort of pinging noise it always makes when she turns it off, almost like the engine isn't quite ready to calm down yet.

"I know what you're thinking," Anna says.

"That's impossible. *I* don't even know what I'm thinking."

"You're thinking it's totally ridiculous for me to get worked up about this, that it was just a forehead kiss."

"I don't think it's ridiculous for you to get worked up about it." I'm not lying—I don't think it's ridiculous. If I were her, I'd probably be getting worked up about it too. I mean, a guy she's been secretly in love with since, like, forever, kisses her? Even if it's just on the forehead, it's still something to get crazy over. It's not like Nico goes around kissing her on the forehead every single day. This is definitely a new development.

"Good," Anna says. "Because I swear, Harper, there was something behind it. It was like, I don't know, *tender* or something. Like he wanted to do more but he was afraid."

I perk up. Now we're getting somewhere. It's definitely possible that Nico wanted to do more but was afraid of freaking

Anna out or messing up their friendship. Although. I did read this magazine article once that basically said guys are pretty much never afraid of ruining friendships the way girls are, and that if they want a girl, they'll go for it no matter what. It was backed up with some kind of scientific study or poll or something. But whatever. Who really listens to magazine articles anyway?

"So, what are you going to do?" I ask. "Just ignore it?"

"I don't know." Anna reaches out and pulls at the fluffy pink steering wheel cover she bought a few months ago during one of our epic all-day mall trips. "I know I should."

"Why?"

"Because it's easier."

"True. But sometimes the easiest thing isn't always the best thing."

"What do you think I should do?" Anna asks.

"I don't know."

"But if you were me, what would you do?"

I don't say anything for a second and instead just look through the windshield at all of our classmates wandering around on the grass. Some of them are laughing, some of them are scowling, some of them look completely indifferent to what's going on. I think about how each of them has a story, something inside themselves they're keeping hidden from the world. I think about Penn, and how he still hasn't told me anything else about his shoulder, how even though we've spent almost every second together for the last few weeks, everything is still so surfacey.

"I think you should tell Nico," I say to Anna.

She turns to me. "You do?"

I nod. "Yeah. I think you should tell him how you feel."

"What if things get weird between us?" she asks.

I shrug. "If things get weird between you, then they get weird between you. But at least you'll know."

"At least I'll know," she repeats softly.

A niggling thought tugs at the back of my mind, telling me that sometimes knowing isn't the best thing. But I push it away. Because sometimes you have to take chances, no matter what you might risk losing.

Penn

Jackson comes up to me before homeroom.

I'm standing at my locker, waiting for Harper, and when I see him, it's like a punch to my gut. I haven't talked to Jackson since the whole incident at the Sailing Burrito—or, as I like to call it, Glassgate.

"Here," he says, slamming a Post-it up against my locker. "You're welcome, even though you don't fucking deserve it."

There's a phone number written on the paper, along with a date and time. *Saturday, 9:30 a.m.*

Has Jackson gotten me a date? We used to have a scheme we'd run, where one of us would go up to a cute girl and tell her the other one wanted her number. The one who wanted the number would stand in the corner and give the girl a timid little smile, like we were too shy to approach her on our own. It was actually very effective. Not only would we get the number, but we'd have the girl thinking we were the kind of guys who didn't do that type of thing very often, when in reality we did it constantly.

"I have a girlfriend," I say, ripping the note off my locker. The words sound foreign coming out of my mouth. Is Harper my girlfriend? I've never really had a girlfriend before. But we're spending almost every second together, so then what else can she really be? "And besides, nine thirty is a little early for a date."

"Don't be an asshole," Jackson says. "It's a doctor's number. You have an appointment at nine thirty on Saturday. And again, you're welcome."

My pulse speeds up, and I look at the Post-it, resisting the urge to crush it with my fist and toss it onto the ground. "Dr. Marzetti?" I ask.

"What?"

"Is the appointment with Dr. Marzetti?" I can't help it, but hope blooms in my chest. Is it possible that somehow Jackson has gotten me an appointment with her? Jackson's dad is rich, and he knows people. Maybe he pulled some strings. Maybe he was somehow able to—

"Who's Dr. Marzetti?" Jackson asks.

I shrug. "No one. Just this doctor I've heard of who does shoulders."

"Well, whatever. This guy's name is Dr. Tamblin, and he's one of the best orthopedic surgeons in the country."

I've heard of him. He does a lot of work on shoulders, yes, but he doesn't specialize in sports medicine. He works more on people who've experienced trauma to their limbs—car accidents, that kind of thing. But I don't want to get into all of that with Jackson. In fact, I don't want to talk to him at all. I just want him to go away. You'd think he'd know that, after I almost threw a glass at his head the other night. But he apparently didn't get the hint. Because he keeps talking.

"I know he doesn't do much sports medicine, but he said he might be able to help you."

I look down at the paper again, the phone number and time staring back at me in Jackson's familiar handwriting. I never told him exactly what was wrong with my shoulder. Maybe my parents told his parents. Or maybe my coach told the team. I don't know how everyone found out or what exactly they were told. I don't even know if Jackson knows enough about what's wrong with me to even know if this doctor can help.

"Thanks," I say, shoving the note into my pocket.

"That's it?" he asks. "Just thanks?"

I shrug. "You did me a favor, so I said thanks. What more do you want from me? I didn't ask you to do that."

Jackson shakes his head, his eyes blazing. "You're a real fucking asshole, you know that, Mattingly?"

Then he turns and walks away. I watch him go, angry at him for giving me that number, angry that it's something I have to think about now. Why can't everyone just mind their own fucking business? I'm not a charity case.

"Hi!" Harper says, bounding down the hall toward me.

She looks cute today. She's wearing a light blue T-shirt and a pair of khaki shorts that show off her long legs. But the good mood I was in this morning when I thought about seeing her is gone.

"Sorry," she says, leaning in and giving me a kiss. "Anna was having drama. Actually, I can probably talk to you about it. You're a guy. If a girl liked you, would you want her to tell you? Even if you were good friends with her?"

I have no idea what she's talking about, and if I'm being completely honest, I don't care. I can't really concentrate on whatever it is she's saying. All I can think about is why Jackson would think it was okay to do something like that. I mean, calling a doctor and making an appointment for me? Isn't that against the law?

"Hello," Harper says. She bumps her hip against mine playfully. But I'm not in a good mood, and my thoughts are racing. "Earth to Penn, I asked you a question."

"Listen, I need to get out of here," I say.

She bites her lip, and her eyebrows knit together in a frown. "Where are you going?"

"I don't know." I open my locker back up and throw my books inside, then slam it shut. "I just . . . I need to get out of here."

"Okay." She shifts her weight from foot to foot. "You want me to come with you?"

"No." I shake my head. "It's fine. I just can't deal with

school today, you know?" I give her a smile so she knows it's not about her, but everything inside me feels jumpy like I want to crawl out of my skin.

I give her a quick kiss on the cheek.

"Okay," she says again. But I can tell she's worried. I give her another quick kiss and then head down the hall.

"Harper," I say as I go, "I'm fine. I promise."

And as I say the words, I almost believe them.

Harper

I watch Penn leave school, wondering what the hell just happened. He sounded fine when he was texting me earlier. But then something must have happened. The look in his eye just now almost reminded me of the night we saw Jackson at the Sailing Burrito.

Speaking of Jackson, I can see him down the hall joking around with some of his baseball friends. They're all huddled in a group, probably talking about something stupid like what girls they want to have sex with. I have a vague memory of some dumb list that was circulated last year, with a bunch of girls ranked on it according to how fuckable they were, and I'm pretty sure the baseball team was the group behind it.

I watch them for a few minutes, marveling at how relaxed

they are. They walk and move with the confidence of guys who are used to things being easy. I remember how Penn told me about how he used to go down to the nurse and she would just let him go home, and I wonder what it would be like to cruise through life like that, to just be able to have things come easily and not worry or obsess about whether or not things were going to work out.

I try to imagine Penn in their little group, try to imagine him walking with that kind of ease, but it's impossible. Penn can be funny and flirty and light. But there's always a little bit of darkness lurking underneath him, just waiting to spill out.

After a few more moments Jackson fist bumps a couple of other guys and then starts walking down the hall. He passes by me, and as he does, he gives me a little nod of acknowledgment.

I hesitate.

Don't do it, Harper. If Penn wanted you to know what was going on with him, then he would have told you. Mind your own business.

But I can't.

It's too late.

The idea's already in my head and it's impossible to stop.

"Jackson," I call.

He turns around, a smile on his face, probably because he thinks it's some girl who wants to hook up with him.

When he sees it's me, his smile fades, but only for a second.

"Hey," he says. He's still smiling, but he also looks a little bit suspicious, like he doesn't know what I'm up to. I don't blame him. The last time I saw him and Penn together, Penn almost threw a glass at his head.

"Hi," I say. "Um, I'm not . . . I mean, you don't have to tell me if you don't want to, but . . . what happened between you and Penn?"

I hold my breath, knowing that what I'm doing is wrong. Obviously something bad happened between Penn and Jackson, and the fact that I'm going behind Penn's back and asking about it isn't that cool. I would be livid if something happened with me and Anna and he did that.

But if Jackson thinks that what I'm doing is wrong or inappropriate, he doesn't show it. In fact, he seems almost curious. "Just now?"

"Just now? Something happened just now?" Well, that would explain why Penn got all dark and just took off.

"Yeah, I got him an appointment with a doctor, and he wigged out." He shrugs. "I guess he thought I should be minding my own business."

"A doctor?"

"Yeah, for his shoulder." He shrugs again. "I know it's probably a long shot, but I figured why not?"

I swallow. Why didn't Penn just tell me that?

"Look, I don't want to cause problems with you and Penn," Jackson says. He sounds like he's telling the truth, which is a contrast to the two other times I've run into him. Once at the batting cages, and once at the Sailing Burrito. Both of those times he seemed like a jackass who didn't give a shit about anything but himself. Now he seems like he's actually concerned about Penn.

"Yeah," I say. "What . . . I mean, what happened between you guys? You know, to make you stop being friends?" I know I'm not supposed to be asking, but I can't help myself. Now that I have someone here in front of me, someone who might know something about Penn, someone who is willing to give me at least a little information, it's too much of a temptation to resist.

"We're not friends anymore." His jaw tightens.

"Yeah, well, that's pretty obvious. But why?"

"You'd have to ask him that."

"He won't tell me."

"Yeah, well, that makes two of us." Jackson's cocky attitude is totally gone now, and he sounds sort of defeated. I can see the pain on his face, and I get it. He misses Penn. He misses the two of them being friends, and anything else I've gotten from him—the cockiness, the douchiness—was him just trying to cover up what was really going on.

"What do you mean, that makes two of us?" I ask.

"Look, after Penn got hurt, everything changed. He didn't want to hang out, he didn't want to be with me, he blew off my phone calls. He just stopped talking to me. And when I tried to force it, it was like he got ridiculously mad at me." He shakes his head. "You saw what happened the other night."

I nod. "So then why'd you give him the name of a doctor?"

"Why wouldn't I?"

"Because he's being a total asshole to you."

"Look, Harper. Penn's the best friend I've ever had. And so I'm going to do whatever I can to help him. Just because he's being douchey to me doesn't change anything."

I nod. The bell rings then.

"I should go," he says. He squeezes my arm. "Take care of him, okay?" he says. And then he disappears into the throng of kids.

"I'm trying," I want to say.

I'm really trying.

Penn

I go to the batting cages.

I go to the batting cages, and I wail on a bunch of balls until my shoulder is screaming.

Every time I hit one, I think about how I got hurt. I think about sliding into home plate, I think about the way I heard my shoulder pop, I think about how I thought it was just dislocated, I think about Jackson showing up today with that dumb doctor's number.

Slam.

Why does everyone have to keep trying?

Slam.

Why does Harper even want to be around me, when I'm such a mess?

Slam.

Why doesn't Jackson just go away, after all the shit I've put him through?

Slam.

Why do people keep pretending there's hope when there isn't? *Slam, slam, slam.*

I don't understand why everyone can't just leave me alone, why people won't just give up on me when I've obviously given up on myself.

When I'm pouring sweat and my shoulder's throbbing, I throw my bat down onto the ground and then gather up my stuff.

When I get home, the house is empty. I pour myself a glass of chocolate milk, then head to the bathroom and take a shower, letting the hot water soothe my muscles.

When I'm done, I think about calling Harper. I know it was wrong of me to just leave her there, standing in the hallway. But I can't be fake with her. She would have known something was up, and she would have asked me what it was, and I didn't—still don't—want to talk about it, so I had to get out of there.

I dress in a pair of jeans and a black T-shirt, then go to my backpack and pull out the Post-it that Jackson gave me this morning.

The number stares back, taunting me.

I hate that he did it, and yet I love it at the same time.

The thing about Jackson is that if he stopped trying, I'd probably fall apart. I don't want to think there's hope for me, and yet I need to know *he* does. It doesn't make sense, I know. But it is what it is.

There's the sound of footsteps coming down the stairs, and I already know who it is before I turn around.

Braden.

His hair is messed up and his eyes are bloodshot.

"Hey," he says, grinning. Say what you want about my brother, but at least he's usually happy to see me. Which is more than I can say for most people.

"Hey," I say. "I didn't know anyone else was home."

He shrugs, like he doesn't care who's here and who isn't. Which he probably doesn't, which is actually good for me. He's not going to ask me any questions about why I'm home in the middle of the day and not at school.

"Whatcha doin'?"

"Nothing." I shove the Post-it note into my pocket. "What are you doing?"

"Just woke up."

"Cool."

"Hey, we should hang out," he says, his eyes brightening. "Yeah, yeah, we should do something fun."

"Yeah, well, I'm not really in the mood for something fun."

"Why not? You having a rough day?"

"Yeah, you could say that."

Braden nods, like he knows all about rough days, even though from what I can tell he has no stress in his life whatsoever. He has no job, no plans, no obligations or responsibilities.

He leans in close to me, like he's about to let me in on a secret. "Know what I do when I have a bad day?" he asks.

I have no idea, because like I said, I had no idea he even had bad days. I wonder what Braden would consider a bad day. Someone beats him in one of his video games? I've heard him in his room at night, on his headset, talking shit to strangers while he plays. "You asshole!" he screams. "Get the fuck out of here! You suck!"

"What?"

He lowers his voice. "I. Get. Fucked. Up."

I consider it. "Sorry," I say. "Pot isn't my thing." It isn't either. The couple of times I've smoked pot haven't been the best. I wasn't mellow, I wasn't relaxed. I didn't like the feeling of being out of control, and I got all paranoid. Plus I hate any kind of smoking. Inhaling stuff into my lungs always gives me the sensation that I can't breathe, which I hate.

"Not pot," Braden says, rolling his eyes like I'm a neophyte. "Tequila."

I look at him. "You have tequila?" I don't know why I'm shocked. The kid has marijuana, of course he's going to have tequila.

"I have all kinds of things," Braden says ominously. He waggles his eyebrows up and down, like maybe he wants me to ask him what else he has. It sounds like he's talking about things that have nothing to do with drugs and alcohol. What else could "all kinds of things" mean, though? Porn? A blow-up doll? The possibilities are endless and scary and I don't want to know.

"Well, whatever," I say quickly. "I don't want to just sit around here and get drunk. That's way too depressing."

"Then let's go out," Braden says. "There's a field party tonight."

I shake my head. "I don't think I'm in the mood to be around anyone." But even as I'm saying the words, I'm thinking, *Why not?* I avoid parties as a rule, because usually the baseball team is there. Also, when I was actually playing, I had too many nights when I'd go out partying, end up a little tipsy, and hook up with some random girl. It gets old fast. On the other hand, what else am I going to do tonight? *Hang out with Harper,* a voice whispers. I ignore it.

"Aww, come on," Braden says. "What else are you going to do?"

Good point.

"Fine," I say. "What time are we going?"

He shrugs, like time has no place in his world.

"Okay. I'm going to be in my room. Come get me when it's time."

I head upstairs and flop down onto my bed. I think about texting Harper just to tell her I'm okay. But I know if I do that, she's going to come back with a ton of questions, and what am I really going to say? That I flipped my lid because Jackson got me an appointment with a doctor? I don't think so.

I turn my phone over and over in my hand, still thinking about it.

Suddenly I feel exhausted.

I close my eyes, and a second later I'm asleep.

Harper

He doesn't even text me.

Not even one text, just to say, "Oh, Harper, I'm so sorry I left you standing there in the hallway like an idiot this morning, but don't worry, I'm okay and I'll make it up to you."

Nothing.

Not one text!

I can't decide if I'm mad or worried. First I'm worried. But then I get mad.

I mean, what's more likely? That he got into some kind of crazy car crash, or that he's just disappeared? What is it that they say? That the best prediction of future behavior is the past? And going by Penn's past behavior, I'd say it's pretty clear that he probably just disappeared.

I make it through the school day, but by that night I'm in a very, very, *very* bad mood. It's made even worse by the fact that I've somehow been convinced by Anna to go to a field party.

"I hate field parties," I grumble as Anna pulls her car into the clearing.

"Why?" she asks. "What's not to like?"

"Oh, I don't know, the fact that there are mosquitoes, and it's dark, and everyone's completely drunk and you always have to worry about whether or not the cops are going to come and haul you down to the police station."

"First of all, it's not that dark. There's always a bonfire. And second, if the cops come, they never haul you down to the police station. They just make sure no one's completely falling-over drunk, and then they tell you to go home."

"Whatever," I mutter as I get out of the car.

"How do I look?" Anna asks, smoothing her dress down. She's wearing a tight red minidress, high sandals, and a pair of long dangly gold earrings. She's way overdressed for a field party. She looks like she's going to a club. But I'm not going to tell her that, because Anna has decided that tonight's the night she's going to tell Nico she's secretly in love with him. Well. Maybe she's not going to tell him that *exactly*. I think it's going to be more like she's going to confess that she likes him as more than a friend.

"Is this dress too much?" Anna asks.

Yes. But I can't tell her that. It's too late to go home and change. And besides, she does look pretty sexy. "No," I say. "You look great. Now just relax."

"Just relax," Anna repeats, blowing out a big breath. She glances around the clearing, where a bunch of cars are parked next to hers. "Do you think he's here yet?"

"I don't know." I glance around. "I don't see his car. Did you text him?"

"Yeah. He said he'd be here soon, and that was a little while ago."

We start traipsing down the path to where the party is.

"I better not get bit up," I grumble. "You know how mosquitoes love me."

"How are you going to get bit up?" Anna calls. She's already a few feet ahead of me, which makes no sense. How is she able to walk so fast in those shoes? "You're all bundled up."

It's true. I'm wearing a pair of jeans and a hoodie over a tank top. It's not that hot out tonight. It rained earlier, and even though it's humid, there's a bit of a chill in the air.

We're getting closer to the clearing now, and a leaf falls from a tree and lands in my hair. I pick it out, irritated. Who decided that having parties in fields was a good idea? Obviously some jerk who wanted to be able to get drunk and couldn't wait until someone's parents went away for the weekend like normal people.

When we get to the spot where the party's taking place, there are about thirty or forty kids already there, hanging out, holding frosty cans of beer procured from coolers. Music drifts from a portable speaker, and everyone's talking and laughing. Ugh. I'm so not in the mood for happiness.

"Do you see him?" Anna asks anxiously. She stands on her tiptoes and scans the crowd.

"No," I say. "But that doesn't mean he's not here. Who can see anything?" I'm just being cranky, because my eyes are already starting to adjust to the darkness. The moon is shining down into the clearing, and, as promised, there's a bonfire casting light around the party. Soon I can make out people's actual features, instead of just figures.

And that's when I see Penn.

At first I squint my eyes, because I'm so shocked that he's there. In the whole time I've been with him, I've never heard him even mention wanting to go to a party. It was one of the things I loved about him—that even though he seemed so dangerous and dark, he seemed happiest when we were just together, at my house, hanging out, doing nothing.

At least, that's what I thought. But now he's standing there, a can of beer in his hand. He's talking to someone. A girl. She's not anyone I recognize, but she looks young, like a freshman or a sophomore. She's tall and curvy, and she has the kind of hair where you can't tell if it's extensions or not because it's so long and curled perfectly.

Penn says something to her, and she laughs and throws her head back. As she does so, her hand turns a little bit, and the fire glints off the delicate silver bracelet she's wearing around her wrist.

She looks put-together and confident, exactly the kind of girl I'm not.

It feels like a rubber band is squeezing my rib cage, and for a second I can't breathe. The party seems to suddenly fade away, and all I can see is Penn and that girl.

Is that why he hasn't texted me? Because he was with her? Is he dumping me for someone else?

At that moment he looks up, and his eyes meet mine.

He doesn't even have the decency to look guilty.

I turn around and start to run.

"Harper!" Anna calls. "What the hell? Where are you going?"

I don't know where I'm going. I just know that I need to get out of here. I'm halfway down the path when I hear someone calling my name. At first I think it's Anna. But then I realize it's Penn.

"Harper!" he says. "Jesus, Harper, slow down."

But I don't. Instead I speed up.

But he's too fast for me, and he catches up a second later. He reaches out and grabs at the sleeve of my hoodie, but I pull away. "Don't touch me," I say.

"Harper," he says, "Come on, stop. Let's talk."

This makes me laugh. I stop and whirl around. "Let's talk? Seriously, did you really just say that?"

He shrugs. "Yeah."

"*Now* you want to talk? Now that you got caught?"

He frowns. "Caught?"

"Yeah." My pulse is racing, and my skin feels flushed. I never knew that anger and emotion could manifest itself in such a physical way.

"Caught doing what?"

"Caught talking to that girl."

"Who?"

"Stop acting like you don't know what I'm talking about!" My fists are balled at my sides, and I can feel the nails cutting into my skin.

"You're talking about Devi? That blond girl? She's in my science class. Harper, we were just talking. Come here."

He reaches for me, but I push him away. I can't take it anymore. I can't take him being close and then pushing me away. I want him so badly, I want to be close to him always. And for him to not want me back, in every single way, the way that I want him, is too much to take.

"No!" I start to walk away from him as fast as I can.

He doesn't say anything or try to stop me, but I can hear his footsteps behind me. It's not until I've gone a few yards that I realize I'm going down the path the wrong way. I'm moving deeper into the woods instead of heading back toward the car and the parking lot.

I don't know what to do. I don't want to turn around, because he's still behind me and that would be humiliating. But I'm not super-excited that I'm heading into the woods either. The last thing I want is to end up getting lost, or attacked by some animal or something.

Penn stops me from making the decision.

"You're going the wrong way," he calls after me.

"I know!" I yell back.

We keep walking. I pray that he doesn't stop following me, because I really don't want to be out here without him. Outside the clearing the moon is more obscured by the trees, and there's obviously no bonfire. I can still hear the voices of my classmates, so at least I know I'm not too far away.

Now that I've slowed down a little bit, my anger is starting to fade.

So when Penn runs to catch up with me, I let him.

He falls into pace beside me.

He doesn't say anything for a few minutes.

"How deep into the woods are we going to go?" he asks finally. "Because if this is going to turn into some kind of *Blair Witch Project* shit, then I need to know about it."

"What's *The Blair Witch Project*?"

He looks at me, stunned. "You never saw *The Blair Witch Project*?"

I shake my head.

"It's one of those found-footage movies. You know, where the people die and they find the footage a little later? A creepy witch kills them in the woods."

"Sounds ridiculous."

"It's not. It's scary."

"Well, whatever," I say. "Stop if you want." I'm praying he doesn't take me up on it. If he leaves me out here alone, I'm going to freak out.

"Nah," he says. "I can't leave you by yourself."

I don't say anything for a few more steps. "I'm still really mad at you."

"Harper," he says, and his voice is soft and sweet. "I swear there is nothing going on between me and that girl. I was talking to her for, like, five minutes."

I stop and whirl around until I'm facing him. "Why didn't you tell me what happened between you and Jackson?"

His jaw tightens. "I don't know what you're talking about."

"He said he got you an appointment for your shoulder." I know I'm taking a risk—there's a chance Penn might completely flip out on me for talking to Jackson behind his back, and he might get even more mad that I'm questioning him about his shoulder.

And for a second I think that's what he's going to do. His jaw tightens even more, and his shoulders square, and he takes a big deep breath through his nose. I can practically see the internal battle going on inside him. Does he stay here and talk to me, or does he tell me to fuck off and take off through the woods? But what am I supposed to do? Just pretend that Jackson didn't tell me any of those things?

Penn lets out the breath he's been holding in. "Can we sit down?" he asks.

"Where? We're in the middle of the woods."

He glances around until he finds a log that looks reasonably stable. We both sit down, and Penn swallows hard and then runs his fingers through his hair. "Jackson got me an appointment at a doctor for tomorrow."

"I know," I say. "He told me."

"I know," he says. "You just told me that."

"So are you going to go?"

He shakes his head. "No."

"Why not?"

"Because, it . . . it doesn't matter. My shoulder is fucked."

"Okay." I think about it. "But how do you know?"

"Because that's what the doctors told me." He reaches for my hand and envelopes one of mine in both of his. I scoot closer to him on the log, suddenly feeling like I want to be as close to him as I can.

"But you haven't talked to this doctor, right?" I say gently.

"No." He shrugs. "But I don't care."

The clouds slip away from the moon then, and his face gets bathed in light. I can see the defensiveness in his eyes. And I realize what it is, why he doesn't want to go to the doctor. He doesn't want to have belief. He doesn't want to think that maybe someone will be able to help him. Because if it turns out they can't, Penn will have to really accept that he won't ever play baseball again. And he's already worked so hard to do that. He doesn't want to have to go through it all over again.

"I think you do care," I say softly. "You know, if you go to the doctor, it doesn't mean anything. It's just an appointment."

He doesn't say anything.

"If they can't help you, you haven't lost anything," I say. "Don't you think you owe it to yourself to explore every possibility?"

He still doesn't say anything. He just kicks at a pebble with his shoe, then pulls me in close to him. I lean against his shoulder, breathing in his scent—peppermint and Axe body wash and clean-smelling laundry detergent. We sit like that for what feels like forever.

I'm not going to push him. Whatever Penn has going on is something he's going to have to work through himself. I can encourage him, but I can't change him. He has to believe he's worth it. He has to believe that if he lets himself think his shoulder can get better and then it doesn't work out, that the disappointment he's going to have to deal with is better than not knowing.

And then, just when I'm letting go of any hope that anything I've said can make a difference to how he feels, the universe decides that maybe I've learned that lesson.

"You'll go with me?" he whispers softly. "Tomorrow? To the appointment?"

"Of course." I say it like it's a given, like it's no big deal.

"Thanks." He kisses me then, his lips warm and soft and sweet, and we sit there, not talking, until finally we get up and he takes me home.

Penn

I used to get nervous before big games.

Once I was out on the field, I was fine. I could stare down a 3–2 count and not even blink. I could be down 0–2 and still go for the homerun.

But before the game—before the game was a different story. I'd stand in the locker room, bent over the toilet, throwing up whatever it was I'd had for breakfast. I always ate something before a game, because if I didn't, it was even worse. The dry heaves would shake my body as the acid burned my throat.

After I threw up, my stomach would still be in knots and I'd be a total asshole to anyone who attempted to talk to me. My coach knew better than to even try to converse with me right before a game. I'd go to the team meeting and just sit there in the corner, in my own little world, trying to keep myself from puking again.

But then, once I stepped onto the grass, everything would change. It was like I got into some kind of zone. Between innings I'd be in the dugout or the bull pen, laughing and joking around, replacing whatever I'd thrown up that morning by eating bananas and drinking Gatorade.

And that's what I'm hoping is going to eventually happen after I wake up the morning of my doctor's appointment and immediately have to run to the bathroom to puke my guts out. At first I'm upset. I mean, who the hell likes to throw up? But then I'm kind of relieved. I've been walking around so numb for so long that it's kind of reassuring to know that I can actually feel something again.

After I'm done expelling the contents of my stomach, I take a long, hot shower, trying to calm my nerves. But it doesn't work. The only good thing about this whole situation is that I have an early appointment. Which means I don't have to spend the whole day sitting around, going crazy, trying to figure out exactly how I feel about all of this.

Harper is picking me up.

It doesn't make me feel great that my girlfriend has to pick me up to take me to a doctor's appointment, but I'm way too keyed up to drive. And it's not like my parents or Braden can take me. Braden's license is suspended (something having to do with "reckless driving," which I'm pretty sure involved an incident where he was driving down I-95 while his friends mooned people), and I'm not in any mood to be around my parents.

I've been steering clear of them since our blowup the other night. Not that it's been hard, since they haven't been around, and not like I would tell them anything anyway. No way I want them to know I'm going to this appointment. The more people who know, the more people I'm going to have to tell if things don't work out.

It's bad enough that Harper knows.

When she pulls into my driveway and honks the horn, I'm already standing on my porch waiting for her. The morning is surprisingly chilly and overcast, and she's wearing this soft pink sweater that makes her skin look fresh and clean. I lean over and kiss her, instantly feeling better.

"Hi," she says. "You seem like you're in a good mood."

"I am now," I say, buckling my seat belt. I reach down and move the seat back so that I have more room for my legs.

We drive into Boston, not really talking much. That's one of the things I love about Harper. Most girls—or people in general, really—would feel they had to fill the silence, that they needed to say a bunch of stuff to try to make me feel better, or just make small talk in an effort to relax me. But Harper's not like that. Harper can just *be*. Just her presence is comforting— she doesn't have to say or do anything special.

We park in the garage across from Mass General, then walk across the street to the medical building. The receptionist points us to the sixth floor, room 612, and we cram into the elevator with a bunch of other people. My stomach drops as we fly up through the floors, and I'm not sure if it's because I'm nervous or because that's just what happens in elevators.

Room 612 turns out to be a waiting room for people who need X-rays.

"I've already had X-rays," I explain to the receptionist after I'm done filling out the insurance paperwork. I'm slightly annoyed. I didn't know this was going to be a whole big thing. For some reason I just assumed I'd be whisked right in to sit down with the doctor, that I'd tell him about my condition and let him know what the other doctors said, and then he'd tell me if he could help me or not.

But of course he's going to want to look at X-rays. And I didn't call my other doctor to have the X-rays sent over here.

"Dr. Tamblin likes to have new ones done," the receptionist says cheerfully. "You can take a seat and we'll call you soon." She points to the chairs against the side of the room.

I sit down.

Harper sits down next to me.

My leg starts to jitter. I don't like just sitting here. I feel like I need to keep moving, that if I'm just sitting here like this, I'm going to have too much time to think, too much time to start running through every single possibility of what's about to happen.

"You okay?" Harper asks.

"I'm fine." I pick a magazine up off the table next to me and start flipping through it. Colors go flying by in a blur of ads and articles, but I'm not seeing anything.

215

"Hey." Harper reaches out and puts her hand on mine. I turn and look at her for the first time. "Whatever happens, it's going to be okay."

I want to ask her how she knows that, how anyone can know that, when they call my name.

"Penn Mattingly?" the nurse asks. "We're ready for you."

There's nothing left to do.

I give Harper a kiss.

And then I get up and follow the nurse through the door.

Harper

As soon as Penn disappears with the nurse, my phone starts ringing.

I look down and see Anna's number on my cell. Shit. I texted her last night to tell her I was going home with Penn, but she never replied.

"Hey," I say, making sure to keep my voice quiet so as not to disturb everyone else in the room. Even so, a woman sitting in a chair across from me gives me a little bit of a dirty look. "Sorry I didn't call you last night. It's just that—"

"Harper," she says, and her voice sounds a little . . . strangled.

"Anna?" I ask. "Are you okay?"

"Noooo." She's wailing now.

"What's wrong?" I sit up straight in my seat. "Are you hurt?"

"No, I'm not hurt. At least not physically." She's gone from wailing to full-on sobbing.

"What happened?"

She starts to talk, but she sounds muffled, almost like she dropped her phone or something.

"What, Anna? Anna, I can't hear you!"

She comes back, but she's still fading in and out. ". . . and then we . . . and now he said . . . I can't believe . . . a mistake!" And she's crying again.

"Anna, I can't understand you. You need to slow down."

She starts to talk again, but before I can figure out if I can finally hear her, someone taps me on the shoulder.

I turn around to see the receptionist standing there, looking at me disapprovingly. "You're not supposed to be on your phone in here." She points to a sign that's on the wall. "The cell phones interfere with the medical equipment."

"Oh," I say. "I'm sorry. I didn't know."

She glares at me. "Yeah, well, there are signs all over the place." She tugs on a piece of her hair. "You could kill someone."

I roll my eyes. "I highly doubt I could kill someone just by talking on my cell phone."

"Then why does it say that it interferes with medical equipment?" the girl sitting next to me asks. "Because my dad is in here for a very important heart procedure, and he can't be having his machines interfered with."

"Relax," I say. "Your dad is going to be fine."

"My dad?" Anna yells in my ear. "What are you talking about, Harper?"

"Look, you're going to have to leave this room," the receptionist says. "I'm sorry, but you're being way too loud."

Which isn't even true, but whatever. "Fine." I roll my eyes and then say, "I'll call you right back" to Anna. I hang up on her midwail and then leave the waiting room and head for the elevators.

Once I'm outside the medical center, I call her back. "Hey," I say when she answers. "Sorry about that. I was . . ." I'm not sure if Penn wants me to mention the fact that he's at the doctor's, so I just say, "I was somewhere that I couldn't talk on the phone."

"Like where?" She sounds suspicious. But before I can come up with a plausible answer, she's already talking. "Harper, it was awful. I mean, it was amazing, but it was awful, too."

She's not crying anymore, but I'm still having kind of a hard time hearing her. Her breath is coming in short gasps, and she's sniffling a lot, probably from all the sobbing.

"What was?"

"Last night." She takes a deep breath, and I can tell she's trying to calm herself down. "I told Nico."

Oh my God, oh my God, oh my God. I'm a horrible friend. I completely and totally forgot about the fact that she was planning on telling Nico she liked him last night. "Good for you," I say automatically, before realizing that if she's crying, it probably didn't go so well. "Um, how did it go?"

"Horrible!" she says. "Well, no, that's not true. At first it went amazing."

"I'm confused." I sit down on one of the benches outside and bend my knees, sliding my feet up next to me. The day is still a little drizzly and cold, and I pull my sweater tighter around me. "It was good or it was bad?"

"Harper," Anna says. "I had sex with him." She sounds stunned.

"You had sex with who?"

"Nico."

"You had sex with *Nico*?!"

"Yes. Oh God, Harper. What have I done?" She's about to start wailing again. Yikes. I've never heard her this upset before.

I try to stay calm. Me getting all worked up isn't going to help the situation. Someone has to be the voice of reason here, and obviously it can't be Anna. "Just relax. Now tell me what happened. Start at the beginning."

"Okay." She takes in a deep shuddering breath. "Well, we were at the party, you know? And we were drinking a little bit, and talking, and by the end of the night, all his friends had gone home and it was just us, you know?"

"Okay." So far it doesn't sound bad. In fact, it sounds completely normal.

"And so I told him that I'd been thinking about how I'd freaked out the other day about my music, and how nice he'd been to me."

"Okay . . ." It still doesn't sound that bad. But I'm waiting for the point where this banal story morphs into Nico and Anna having sex and things going horribly wrong. And then amazing? Isn't that what she said? That it was horrible and then amazing? Or was it amazing and then horrible?

"And so he said it was no problem, that he was always going to support me no matter what. So then I said that I really appreciated that, which was one of the reasons I thought he was such a good friend."

"Good." This story really has a slow build. I know I told her to start at the beginning, but does she really need to get into this kind of detail? I hope when she gets to the sex part, she doesn't start getting all into every little thing that happened. The last thing I want to hear is all the details of my best friend losing her virginity. Well, of course I want to hear the details. Just not the way gross ones.

"So then I said that when he kissed me on the head that day, my feelings for him kind of changed."

Now I'm confused. "Why'd you say that?"

"Because you said I should tell him I like him as more than a friend!"

"No, I mean . . . you said that your feelings changed for him when he kissed you. But that's not true. You liked him before that. For a long time."

"Well, yeah, but I didn't want *him* to know that."

Something tells me that Anna beginning her confession by not telling Nico the whole truth probably didn't give her the

221

best chance of starting things off on the right foot. But I'm not going to say that to her. I mean, it's too late now. She can't change it.

"So then what happened?" I ask.

"So then he kissed me. Like, a real kiss. Not on the head. On the mouth."

"Oh my God! Just like that?"

"Yeah." She sighs. "And so then we were kissing some more, and then he asked me if I wanted to go back to his house, and so then I said yes, and then we went back to his house, and his parents were already sleeping and we went into his room and we had sex."

"Wow. So was it . . . I mean, did you like it?" I know I said I didn't want to hear all the details but now I actually sort of do.

"Yeah. I mean, it kind of hurt at first, but then it started feeling really good."

"So then why was it awful?"

Her breathing starts getting all raggedy again. "It . . . it started getting bad this morning. When we woke up, it was all awkward. And, like, his parents were downstairs, so I had to sneak out the back door. And then he called me, and it was just . . . He doesn't . . . I mean, he's not sorry it happened. But basically he doesn't feel the way about me that I feel about him."

"But he had sex with you!"

"Harper, having sex with someone doesn't always mean you have romantic feelings for them." She says it like I should know this, even though the grand total of people I've had sex with is zero.

"I know that," I say, because let's face it, you don't have to be a genius to figure it out. "But it's just weird that he would sleep with you if he didn't at least feel *something*."

"He said that he was attracted to me, but that his feelings weren't that deep. That he wasn't sorry it happened, but that he thought maybe we should try . . . to . . . to just . . . to just go back to being friends." She's sobbing again now.

"Oh, Anna, honey," I say. "I'm so sorry." I understand why she's so upset. And I can also see where the confusion came in. Anna didn't tell Nico that she's had feelings for him for a while, that she's been practically in love with him since the day they met. So when she said her feelings had just changed a couple of days ago, he probably thought it was new and that maybe he should just give it a try. Still. He definitely acted like a douche.

"Can you come over?" she sobs. "I just . . . I don't want to be alone right now."

"Of course," I say. "Just let me finish up what I'm doing."

"How long?" she wails. "Actually, can I come over to your house? I don't want to be at home right now. My mom's here, and I know she can tell something's up. She's so nosey and she might ask me about it, and if she does, I really might crack and tell her. And then she's never going to let me talk to Nico again in my life because she'll . . . she'll . . . she'll hate him."

I'm kind of starting to hate him too. Nico and I were never

that close. The only reason I even hung out with Nico in the first place was because Anna was such good friends with him. But now that I'm thinking about it more, it's actually a pretty shitty thing to sleep with one of your friends and then basically tell them it didn't mean anything to you. I mean, seriously, where does he get off?

"Of course you can come over," I say. "Just let me get home first. I'll call you in a little bit, okay?"

"But how long? Where are you?"

"I'm . . ." I sigh. I don't want to lie to her. And besides, Penn never explicitly said I couldn't tell anyone. "I'm at the hospital. With Penn."

"The hospital?" Anna shrieks. "What happened? Oh my God, you're not pregnant, are you!"

"No, I'm not pregnant. Jesus, Anna. You have to have sex to get pregnant." The words are out of my mouth before I realize that's probably not the best thing to say to her. I mean, she just had sex last night. Oh God. "You used a condom, right, Anna?"

"Of course I used a condom," she says. "What do you think I am, stupid?"

"No, of course not."

At that moment I look up and see Penn walking through the automatic double doors of the hospital. He takes a few steps outside and glances around, probably looking for me.

"Anna," I say. "I'll call you right back."

"No! You can't hang up. I'm freaking out!"

"I'll call you back in five minutes. Actually, just start heading over to my house if you want, okay? I'll meet you there."

I hang up before she has a chance to say anything else. I'm not trying to be a bitch. It's just that Penn is standing in front of me now, and I don't want Anna to overhear whatever it is he's going to say. He has a look on his face that I've never seen before. It's not mad or angry or sad or happy or anything. It's just sort of . . . blank.

"Hey," I say cautiously.

"Hi." He swallows hard.

"Sorry I had to leave. It's just . . . I had an emergency."

He nods, not asking what the emergency is or if I'm okay.

"So how did it go?" I ask.

He shrugs. "They can't help me."

"Oh, Penn, I'm so sorry." I move toward him and reach for his arm, but he shrugs me off.

"It's not a big deal," he says, his voice even. "I just want to go home."

"Yeah, of course." I nod. "I'll take you home. Or . . . do you want to come to my house?" Anna's on her way over, but it's not like I can just leave Penn by himself. He might need me. And besides, misery loves company, right? Maybe we can all sit together and commiserate about how crappy everything feels right now.

But Penn shakes his head. "No. I don't . . ." He swallows again, like it's a big struggle to get the words out. "I think I'm just going to walk around for a while."

"Around Boston?"

"Yeah."

"But . . . I mean, do you want me to go with you?"

"No."

"Penn—"

"Look, Harper, I appreciate you driving me and every-thing, but I just want to be alone for a while."

He turns around and walks away.

Without kissing me.

Without saying he'll call me later.

Without even telling me how he's going to get home.

Penn

I blame her.

I know it's ridiculous and stupid and doesn't make any sense, but I blame Harper. I blame her for bringing me here, for making me take this appointment, for making me believe that maybe something could have changed for me, that I could go back to the life I had before I got hurt.

If I'd never met her, I never would have gone to the stupid appointment.

And if I'd never gone to the stupid appointment, I wouldn't have had to sit there while a doctor I'd never met before looked at my X-rays for ten minutes and then told me that there was nothing he could do for me.

It was a waste of time.

A waste of energy.

A waste of emotion.

My body felt all keyed up after I left there, like I needed to run or get to the batting cages. The problem was, I'd driven into the city with Harper, and so I needed to leave with her. But the thought of sitting in that car while she drove me home, either in tense silence or, worse, with her trying to make me feel better, filled me with anxiety.

I couldn't do it.

So I took off. And now I'm wandering around Boston trying to figure out what the hell I'm going to do. The drizzle from this morning is beginning to burn off, and even though the sun isn't out, it's starting to get hot. I take off the hoodie I'm wearing and drop it into a nearby trash can, not wanting to have to deal with carrying it around.

I walk the streets, hoping to get some energy out, but all it's doing is getting me more worked up. I grab a chicken taco and a Sprite from a Taco Bell, but after two bites and a couple of sips, I toss them out.

The streets are filled with people, all of them enjoying the fact that it's not cold or snowing or raining, which in Boston sometimes feels like a miracle. They're all smiling and laughing and shopping and eating, and they're annoying me. I start to feel like I want to blame them too for what I'm going through, even though I know it's not their fault.

Then I start to think about whose fault it really is.

The doctors.

Harper.

My dad.

Jackson.

Jackson. He's the one who's really responsible for this. He's the one I really should be blaming. As I storm down the streets of Boston, turning this way and that, not really knowing where I'm going, I decide that this whole tack I've taken with Jackson—just shutting down and ignoring him—has got to stop.

I need to confront him.

He needs to pay.

And it needs to be now.

Of course, this whole plan is a lot easier said than done, since I have no car and I'm in the city. But now that the idea's in my head, it won't go away. I have to confront Jackson. I think about calling him and demanding that he come down here and meet me, but if I do that, I'm going to lose the element of surprise.

So I hop on the T, deciding to take it as far as I can and then walk the rest of the way to Jackson's house. The subway ride takes about an hour and a half, and by the time I emerge onto the street, the sun is out in full force. It makes me feel hot but not tired. And before I know it, I'm standing outside Jackson's house. It's a white cape with a dormer on one side, and as I stand on the porch, about to ring the bell, I think about how strange it is to be back here.

When Jackson and I used to be friends, I never would have

bothered ringing the doorbell. I would have just walked in.

I take a deep breath and then knock loudly.

I'm not in a ringing-the-doorbell kind of mood.

No one answers, so I knock again.

And again.

And again.

And again.

Finally I see the curtains by the bay window in the living room twitch, and Jackson peers out, bleary-eyed. He probably just woke up, no doubt because he was out all night partying and messing around with some girl.

I give him a friendly wave and a big fake smile.

"Jesus, Mattingly," he says when he opens the door. "What time is it?"

"Oh, I don't know. Probably, like, noon," I say happily, pushing by him and into the kitchen.

"Come on in," he says, rolling his eyes and shutting the door behind me.

Suddenly I'm inexplicably starving. I open Jackson's refrigerator, nodding in satisfaction when I see that it's filled to the brim. His mom always buys the best food.

"I'm going to have a sandwich," I announce.

Jackson looks alarmed. "Are you okay?" He peers at me. "Are you . . . you're not fucked up, are you?"

"Fucked up?"

"Yeah. On some of that shit Braden's been smoking, or maybe something worse?"

"Oh, no. I'm totally sober. I have a totally clear mind." The first part's true. The second part I'm not so sure about, but whatever. I start pulling lunch meats out of the refrigerator and piling them on the counter. Jackson's family has good lunch meat—all natural and organic, none of those nitrites or fillers. I pull a loaf of pumpernickel bread out of the bread box and start slicing it.

"Help yourself," Jackson says sarcastically, sitting down at his kitchen table. He yawns.

"Thanks. I think I will." I look down at the bread, calculating in my head how much is left. "Would you like a sandwich?" I ask magnanimously.

He looks at me in disbelief. "Sure." He shrugs. "Why the hell not. And can you make some coffee, too? I had a really hard night, and—"

I silence him with a look. "Seriously?"

He shrugs. "Hey, you're the one who showed up at my house, barging in and demanding lunch."

"Really?" I stop with the mustard halfway to my sandwich. "Really? Because if we're going to talk about who inconvenienced who the most, I think I'm going to win that argument."

"Fair enough." He gets up and gets to work making coffee. We bustle around the kitchen for a few moments, not saying anything.

Finally we sit down at the table.

He puts a cup of coffee in front of me, and I put a sandwich in front of him. It's all very strangely domestic.

231

We sit in silence and eat.

"So I'm assuming you're here for more than Saturday breakfast," Jackson says.

"It's lunch, and yes, I'm here for more than that."

"Care to clue me in?"

I shrug. "Well, I was going to come here and beat the shit out of you."

Jackson shakes his head. "I thought you got that out of your system last year." He's talking about the fight we had after I realized I was never going to play again. I went in to clean out my locker. I hadn't planned on ever going back to the locker room, but I didn't want someone else on the team to have to gather my stuff, couldn't bear the thought of someone else having to clear out my things, all the while feeling sorry for me.

I went during a game, when I thought no one would be there. But Jackson was. He was bruised up from what had happened to him during the practice where I got hurt, and so he wasn't playing. He was sitting on the bench, taping up his ankle, and we ended up getting into it. I yelled. He yelled. I punched him. He wanted to punch me back, but he didn't. And it's a good thing too. My shoulder was still sore, and he probably would have kicked the shit out of me.

"Apparently not," I say. This whole fake thing I had going on—coming over here, acting all cheerful, making myself a sandwich—is starting to fade. All the energy I had is dissipating, like a wave washing out to sea, leaving only raw anger in its place.

"Why did you make me that doctor's appointment?" I ask.

Jackson starts dumping sugar into his coffee. He shrugs. "Because I thought it could help."

"Because you thought it could help, or because you felt guilty?"

Jackson shakes his head and for a second I feel like he's going to yell at me. But then he just sighs. "Yes," he says.

"Yes?"

"Yes, Penn. Is that what you want to hear? That I feel guilty for what happened to you? That I feel responsible?"

"I don't want to hear anything. I want to hear the truth." But it's a lie. I don't want to hear the truth. All I want to hear is the carefully constructed narrative that I've been replaying in my head for the past year. The narrative that says that Jackson did it on purpose, that he defended the plate like that just to fuck me up. That because we'd had a fight in the locker room beforehand, he did it just to be a dick.

"You don't want to hear the truth," Jackson says. He's sitting back in his chair now, his food forgotten, his eyes cold. "You only want to hear what you want to hear."

"That's not true. I want you to tell me the truth about what happened."

"Jesus Christ, Penn. I have told you the truth! It was an accident. That shit happens. I'm sorry, and yes, I feel guilty. I feel guilty every fucking day, every fucking time I see you. I think about how if I'd just been one millimeter to the side, if I'd just—"

"If you just hadn't been trying to get back at me!" I yell, and stand up.

"No." Jackson's voice gets quiet, and he looks down at his hands. "No, Penn. I didn't do it on purpose. I feel guilty because I played a part in what happened to you, yes. But I didn't do it on purpose."

He looks back up at me and I can tell—no, I *know*—he's telling the truth. I can see it in his eyes. We've been friends since we were two. I know he's not lying. I let myself feel that for a moment—that it was an accident—but then I stop. I have to believe he did it on purpose. Otherwise it's just one of those things that happen, one of those things you have no control over.

And that's too hard.

It's too painful.

I need someone to blame.

So even though I know he's telling the truth, I shut it down. I close my feelings off, and it's the ugliest, dirtiest part of me that decides to refuse to believe him. So instead of telling him I know he's telling the truth, I say, "You're a fucking liar, Jackson. You're a liar and a coward."

I go to leave, and I can see the anger on his face. He can't believe I showed up here to talk and now I'm calling him a liar and a coward. For a second I can't believe it either. For a second I want to take it back.

But I push that feeling away.

I make myself believe that I don't care if Jackson is pissed. In fact, I make myself believe that I like it.

Harper

Here is what happens the rest of the day:

Anna comes over. At first she is inconsolable. But then she calms down, and we're able to spend the day eating Mexican food (lunch), Chinese food (dinner), and ice cream (dessert and midnight snacks).

I text Penn. He doesn't text me back.

I text him again, saying I don't care if he doesn't want to talk, but to at least let me know he's okay. He texts back *I'm okay* and that's it.

Here is what happens the rest of the weekend:

I work on my audition piece for Ballard, trying to lose myself in the music and the dance. But it doesn't help. I can't stop thinking about Penn. For once I'm actually looking forward to school, because it means I'm going to see him.

But on Monday morning he doesn't come to pick me up. I stand at the window, looking for his car, my stomach rolling with anxiety. I tell myself he's not blowing me off, that he could be sick or maybe having car trouble. I pull my phone out of my pocket, wondering if I should text him. I don't want to seem like a crazy stalker.

Plus, my heart is telling me what I already know. He's not hurt. He's not having car trouble. He just doesn't want to see me. He started to open up, and then he freaked out, and so now he's shutting down. It's classic Penn.

But still, I send him the text anyway.

I hold my breath. But he never replies.

And when it's too late to wait any longer, my mom drives me to school.

In world history Penn walks by my desk without a glance.

"What's up with him?" Anna asks.

I roll my eyes and pretend it doesn't bother me. I know it's stupid after the way he's been treating me, but I still don't want to betray Penn's trust and tell Anna about what happened. I also don't want to have to say the truth out loud, that things might be over between us, that every time Penn gets even remotely close to me, he immediately pulls back.

I shrug. "You know boys," I say.

"Oh, yeah," Anna sighs. "I know boys." She's calmed down a lot after what happened with her and Nico, but she's still crying herself to sleep at night. Which makes sense. I mean, it's only been a couple of days. I haven't seen Nico at all this morning, which is a good thing. In the mood I'm in, I definitely don't trust myself not to go off and tell him exactly what I think of what he did.

I can't concentrate during class, and when the bell rings, I run out of there, not wanting to give Penn another chance to pass by me.

I hear him calling after me when I'm halfway down the hall.

"Harper!"

I know I shouldn't turn around. But I do. "Yeah?"

"Hi." He grins at me.

"You didn't pick me up this morning," I accuse. I'd planned on trying to play it cool, but apparently that isn't going to happen.

"This morning? Yeah, sorry. I was running late."

"Okay." I know he's lying, but I don't have the energy to push him on it. We just stand there, staring at each other. He doesn't reach for my hand, he doesn't apologize for taking off the other day at the doctor's office, he doesn't even tell me anything more about what happened.

"Is that all?" I ask finally.

"Is what all?"

"Well, you called my name. I wasn't sure if there was something you wanted to talk to me about." My words come out more biting than I planned, but I kind of don't care.

The hall is crowded, and we're starting to get jostled

around, so we take a few steps closer to the wall. "Look, do you want to get out of here?" Penn asks.

I stare at him incredulously. "No, I don't want to get out of here."

"Why not?"

"Why not? Because every time something comes up that we should talk about, you can't just decide that we need to cut school!"

He sighs, then moves closer to me and tries to brush his lips against mine.

But I'm pissed. "Seriously, Penn. Are we going to talk about this?"

His eyes get all dark and stormy and broody. "Talk about what?"

"About what happened with the doctor. About Jackson, about your shoulder, about any of it!"

"I told you," he says. "The doctor couldn't help me. And I don't want to talk about it anymore. We've talked about it enough."

"Fine." I know I should let it go, but for some reason I can't. There shouldn't be things we're not allowed to talk about. I don't want to not know things about him. Tears are poking at the backs of my eyes, and I blink hard, not wanting to cry here in the hallway, in front of everyone.

"I don't want to talk about baseball," Penn says. "So come on, Harper. Let's get out of here. I'll buy you lunch. Anywhere you want."

I can feel my anger intensifying. It's like the more he tries to calm me down and pretend nothing's wrong, the madder I get. "Penn, how come we never go to your house?" I demand.

"What?"

"You said you don't want to talk about the baseball stuff, or about your shoulder, or Jackson. Okay, fine, I get it. But how come we never go to your house? How come I know nothing about your family, or where you live?"

"Jesus, Harper," he says. "What is your problem?"

"What's my problem?"

"Yes! You're freaking out over absolutely nothing. Look, I'm sorry I didn't pick you up this morning, but you're acting crazy."

I shake my head. "No, Penn, I'm not. It's not crazy to want to know things about the person you're with. You shut down every time you let me get even a little close, and I'm sick of it."

"Yeah, well, maybe I'm sick of you always pushing me." He shakes his head. "Look, maybe this just isn't working."

The words hang there in the air. This is the part where one of us is supposed to take them back, to say something that's going to change the situation, to stop what it is that's happening. But both of us just stand there.

It needs to be him. He needs to be the one to take it back.

Otherwise it doesn't count.

He's the one who said the words.

He's the one who needs to take them away.

But he doesn't.

"I just . . . maybe we just both need a break," he says.

I stare at him, not sure what to say.

I don't need a break. I don't want a break. In fact, I want the opposite of a break. I want to be close to him, I want us to tell each other everything, I want him to stop holding me at arm's length.

I'm scared to say all that. But I take a deep breath and say it anyway. "I don't want a break," I say. "I want . . . I just want to be together."

His shoulders sort of slump, and I see his face fall and relax. I take a step toward him, and he puts his arms around me, and we stand there in the hallway, just holding each other for a long moment.

"Penn," I whisper into his ear. "Penn, please, you have to let me in."

But then he pulls back and I feel his body stiffen.

He pulls my arms from around him.

He holds my wrists by my sides for a second.

And then he turns around and walks away.

Penn

I walk away.

It's the easy way out, the worst thing I could possibly do to her, but I do it anyway.

I leave school.

I go home.

I don't look back.

I don't think that we're really going to be taking a break. I mean, people have fights. They say things in the heat of the moment that they don't mean, and then they move on. I expect that Harper's going to call me or that maybe she'll write me a funny text later, one that makes light of our fight.

But she doesn't.

I go to the dance studio that night, fully intending to

apologize to her. I watch her through the window as she helps her mom with a lesson, demonstrating dance steps and moving gracefully across the studio. I marvel at how beautiful she is, and wonder why she likes me—why when she could have any guy she wants, she somehow wants to be with me.

I sit there, transfixed as she effortlessly twirls across the floor. Even though I know this isn't the kind of dance she wants to be doing, she looks gorgeous doing it. That's how good she is.

My fists clench in frustration. I want to storm in there, like some kind of crazy last scene of a romantic movie, where the hero comes in and sweeps the heroine off her feet and carries her out the door in front of everyone, finally proving himself.

But how can I? She wants something from me that I can't give her.

She wants me to open up to her, but how can I when I've kept things buried for so long? She wants more than I can give her, more of me than I've ever given to anyone else, even before I got hurt.

I sit there in the parking lot, still resisting the urge to go in.

I will her to look up, to see me sitting out here, to catch my eye and then come outside and demand to know what I'm doing here. And then I could tell her. I could tell her I'm here because I don't want to lose her, that I can't promise everything's going to be okay right away, but that I'll work on it.

But I don't.

I sit there until it gets dark, until Harper leaves the studio and walks right by my car, not even knowing I'm there.

I sit there long after she's gone, telling myself I should call her. I even pull my phone out and pull up her number on my contacts screen.

But I don't call her. Not because I don't want to. But because I'm a coward.

And finally, when all the lights in the plaza have gone off, and I'm the very last car in the parking lot, I pull out and drive home.

Harper

This is how my breakup happens:

Penn doesn't call.

He doesn't text.

He's not in school for the rest of the week, and when he turns up on Monday, he breezes by me in history class like I'm just a girl he's never known, like we didn't spend hours and hours kissing on the chaise lounge on my patio, like we didn't get close, like we didn't spend every moment together.

He acts like he doesn't know me.

"Are you going to tell me what happened finally?" Anna asks on our way out of class.

"I told you," I say. "He couldn't commit. He's a normal guy."

"That's not the whole story," she says.

"It is." Maybe someday I'll tell her about Penn's shoulder, about taking him to the doctor, about all the reasons he shut down. But right now, for some inexplicable reason, I'm still protecting him. Or maybe it's myself I'm protecting, I don't know.

"Well, misery loves company," Anna says, sighing as she looks down the hall to where Nico is standing at his locker.

I resist the urge to roll my eyes. Anna and Nico are somehow back to being friends. They still hang out and text all the time. She still has lunch with him, she still gets to call him anytime she wants and do her homework with him and ask him what he thinks about whatever's on her mind.

I've lost all of those things with Penn. Nothing with Anna and Nico has even changed. It's gone back to exactly the way it was. They still hang out, and she still pretends she's fine with them just being friends.

I want to scream at her, to tell her that it's totally different, her misery and mine. I want to yell at her that she's being just as fake as Penn, that she's not letting her feelings out, and that if you hold everything inside, you end up with broken hearts and misunderstandings.

But I can't. My broken heart is not her fault.

So instead I tell her that I'll see her later, and then I do what I always do after I see Penn in world history.

I go into the bathroom and cry.

The next two weeks pass by in a blur, and I throw myself into my audition piece for Ballard. I practice and practice and practice. My shoulders get sore and my feet ache, but I don't feel any of it. I just keep going, choreographing dance after dance after dance. Not just my audition piece, but other dances as well—hip-hop, freestyle, samba. I even help my mom work with her students Kaitlyn and Jeremy on their wedding dance.

Every time I slow down, all I can think of is Penn. I've gotten good at coming into world history late, keeping my head down as I take my seat, and forcing myself not to look to the back of the room. As soon as the bell rings, I rush out. If I happen to see Penn in the hall, I put my head down and keep going. Out of sight, out of mind.

The morning of my audition is the first time in a long time that I wake up and Penn isn't the first thing I think about. For one amazing second when I open my eyes, I forget that we're broken up. And then it all comes rushing back.

I force myself out of bed.

"Hi," my mom says when I get downstairs. She's holding a bagel smeared with peanut butter on a plate, a glass of orange juice, and a cup of coffee.

"Hi." I shake my head at the food. "I'm too nervous to eat."

"You have to eat something." She puts the food down on the counter. "You'll have no energy."

"I have a ton of energy."

"You need fuel. Come on, humor me."

I sigh and take the plate, nibbling at the bagel.

"Are you sure you don't want me to drive you?" my mom asks. "I'm happy to do it."

"I'm positive. You know I need to get into a zone." I don't like anyone around me when I'm doing something I know is going to be high stress. I like to get hyper-focused and tune everything out. I don't like any distractions, especially not people trying to talk to me.

"Okay." She pauses, and I can tell she's worried about me. She knows that Penn and I broke up, but she doesn't know the reasons why. She didn't ask, and I didn't offer. It's another reason I hate him—he has infected every part of my life, to the point where he's now even affecting my relationship with my mom.

My mom reaches over and smoothes my hair down. "You're going to do great," she says. "You're going to be amazing. And if they don't see that, you'll find a place that will."

"Thanks." I know she's just saying that because she has to. For me there's never been anything but this. I need to get into the choreography program. If I don't, I don't want to even *go* to Ballard. I'll have to take a year off and try again, or maybe go to community college and hope my credits will transfer. I have my first flash of what Penn might be going through when it comes to figuring out college, but I push him out of my mind.

He's not going to get into my head today.

He's not going to ruin this for me.

I won't let him.

Penn

It's been three weeks since I talked to Harper, three weeks since I kissed her, or touched her, or heard her voice. Every day I watch her come into world history, her head down, making sure not to look at me. It's obvious what she's doing. She used to be one of the first ones to come into class, and now she's one of the last. Initially I hated that she wouldn't look at me. But now I like it. It's the one moment of my day when I can see her and not have to feel bad about it.

It's excruciating not to talk to her.

I want to, but with every day that goes by, it gets harder and harder.

So on Wednesday, when she doesn't come into world history, I have a slight moment of panic. Why isn't she in class? Is she sick? Is she okay?

I look at Anna, who's texting on her phone, holding it under her textbook so the teacher won't notice. She doesn't look too concerned, so I let out the breath I've been holding. If something were wrong with Harper, Anna wouldn't be acting like nothing was wrong.

And then I spot the date on the board.

The fourteenth.

Today's Harper's audition, the one for the choreography program.

My heart speeds up, and I pull out my phone, wondering if I should send her a text and wish her good luck, let her know I'm thinking of her. But what if she doesn't text me back? This is definitely one of those rare times when a phone call is better than a text. I raise my hand and ask for the bathroom pass.

On the way out of the room, I swear Anna gives me a suspicious look, like she knows I'm going to call Harper. She glares at me, almost like she's telling me not to ruin this for Harper. But there's no way she could possibly know what I'm up to, and she's probably just giving me the normal look that girls give guys who've totally fucked over their best friends.

But still.

It's enough to make me pause when I get out of the class-room and into the hallway. What if I screw her up? What if Harper's just about to go into her audition and I call her and she gets all distracted and flubs the whole thing? I stare down at my phone, trying to remember if there was a specific time she was supposed to start. She might not be dancing yet.

I'm just standing there, staring down at my phone like an idiot, when it rings in my hand.

Harper.

It's my first thought.

But it can't be.

The number is one I don't recognize, and if it were her, her name would have come up on my caller ID. But what if she's calling from someone else's phone? What if her phone died and she had to borrow one? It's a ludicrous story that I've totally fabricated in my head like some kind of psycho, but I've almost convinced myself it's true.

"Hello?" I say when I answer, half expecting to hear her voice.

"Hello. Can I speak with Penn Mattingly, please?" a female voice asks. But it's not Harper.

"This is Penn," I say, before realizing that you should always ask who it is before you admit to who you are.

"Hi, Penn. This is Diana from Dr. Marzetti's office," she says. "I'm calling because Dr. Tamblin referred you to us. Dr. Marzetti has a cancellation, and I'm wondering if you'd like to take the appointment?"

I'm about to tell her no, that I'm not in the market for a doctor right now and she can take me off her list. But something stops me. "When is the appointment?"

"At noon."

"What date?"

"Today."

"Today?"

"Yes, Mr. Mattingly," she says, like she can't believe I would be shocked. "As you can tell, it's very short notice, so if you don't want to take it, please let me know so that I can call the next person on the list."

Wow. This chick has a serious attitude. I wonder if it's because she's on some kind of power trip because she works for a powerful doctor. She's probably used to people falling all over themselves to rush down to the hospital whenever she snaps her fingers. Maybe she even get bribes, like people sending her presents so she'll schedule an appointment for them. Well. If she thinks she's going to get that kind of treatment from me, she has another thing coming.

"I'll be there," I say, shocking myself. "Thanks for calling."

"See you then. And please have any X-rays or medical records e-mailed over before you come." She rattles off the e-mail address, which I immediately forget. But that's the least of my worries.

The most of my worries is that I've somehow agreed to go to a doctor's appointment in an hour. Not that leaving school is a problem. It will be the first time I've left school in the middle of the day for an actual legit reason, ha-ha.

Why did I do that? I wonder, still staring at my phone. Why would I agree to go to that appointment?

Harper.

Her name pops into my head again before I can stop it. But why would I go because of Harper? Because I want an excuse to call her. And if I go to this doctor, and she tells me something I want to hear, or even something I don't, I'll have one. But I want to call her now. I want to call her and tell her I'm going to the doctor, that I'm ready to talk to her, that I want to let her in, that I miss her so much, it hurts.

But I stop myself.

If I call her now, it's not going to mean anything. What am I going to say? Oh, I have a doctor's appointment? No, I decide. It will be better once I'm done, once I actually have something concrete to tell her.

I don't even bother going back to history to get my books.

I just take a deep breath. And tell myself I'm ready to face this.

The receptionist at Dr. Marzetti's office is nothing like I pictured her. I thought she'd be kind of older—like, thirty—with a pinched-up face. Instead she looks like she's in college, and she has long shiny brown hair, and she gives me a big smile when she sees me.

"You must be Penn," she says. "It's nice to put a face with the name." If I didn't know better, I'd think she was flirting with me. And if I wasn't so hung up on Harper, I'd probably flirt back.

"Yup," I say. "That's me."

She hands me a clipboard with a form on it and asks me to fill it out. "And did you have your X-rays e-mailed over?"

"Yes." I found Dr. Marzetti's e-mail address on their

website, then called Dr. Tamblin on the way over here and asked them to send the X-rays.

"Okay," she says, giving me another warm smile. "I'll let the doctor know you're here. It shouldn't be that long."

I take a seat in the waiting room and start filling out the form. There's only one other person in here, a man with a buzz cut and broad shoulders who's flipping through a magazine. I'm finished filling out the form in about three minutes, and the receptionist isn't back yet, so I just go and set the clipboard down on her desk.

My leg is jittering up and down, and there's an unsettling feeling in my stomach. It's not the same kind of feeling I'd get before a game, not the nauseous I'm-going-to-throw-up feeling. Instead it's something else. Excitement?

I pull out my phone and text Harper.

At an appointment with another doctor. I miss you. A lot.

I hold my breath and stare at the screen, waiting to see if she'll text me back. I tell myself it doesn't mean anything if she doesn't, that she's at an audition, that she might not have her phone on her.

Five minutes later I'm still staring at a blank screen.

"Penn?" the nurse calls, opening the door to the back of the office. "They're ready for you."

Harper

Okay, so the girls at this audition are super hard-core. Like, *really* hard-core. I mean, I know dancers are some of the toughest people out there. You have to be to put your body and mind through everything it takes to be successful at dance. But seriously, these girls are taking it to another level.

They're all wearing expensive dance clothes and eating these energy Shot Blok things, and then they start jumping around and doing complicated-looking stretches. It's honestly making me a little nervous. I mean, these girls have been training and practicing since they were, like, five. And yeah, I know a lot of them aren't really my competition. Most of them are here for other dance programs, not choreography like me. But still.

I turn off my phone, shove my earbuds into my ears, find a quiet corner of the hotel lobby, and start my warm-up.

Penn

The nurse leads me into a small room that looks more like an office than an examination room. There's a big mahogany desk sitting in the middle and a bunch of framed diplomas hanging on the wall, all from impressive-sounding schools, like Harvard, Columbia, and Penn. There's a bunch of awards, too, for patient satisfaction, that kind of thing. On the desk is a picture of two smiling children. One's missing a top tooth, and the other has pigtails. It's such a normal-looking picture that for some reason it makes my heart squeeze.

"Penn?" the doctor asks as she comes into the room. "Hi. I'm Dr. Marzetti."

"Hello." I stand up and shake her hand. She has long blond hair, and she looks a lot younger than I pictured her. I thought in order for her to be the best in her field, she'd have to be at least sixty, but she looks like she's in her early forties.

"So," she says, sitting down. Her voice is warm, but I can tell she's the type who doesn't like to waste any time. "I looked at your X-rays. Baseball player, right?"

"Yes." I nod. "How did you know that? Did Dr. Tamblin tell you?"

She grins. "Dr. Tamblin said you were an interesting case, but he didn't tell me the specifics, just that I might want to give you a call. I can tell by the X-rays, though. Collision at the plate?"

I nod, not saying anything. I don't like the word "collision." Every time I hear it, it makes me relive that moment.

"So," she says, "there are a couple of things we can do. But I want to make sure you—"

I shake my head. "What?"

"About your shoulder. There are a couple of things we can do. The first one is riskier, but it's—"

"Wait, hold on." I lick my lips and swallow hard. "How do you . . . I mean, don't you have to take more X-rays?"

She looks down at the chart in front of her. "You just had these done recently, right?"

I nod again, not trusting myself to talk. My heart is pounding, and I can practically hear the blood rushing through my body.

"Then, no, you don't need new ones. There's very little change from the ones you had before, anyway, when you first got hurt. The bone is healed, yes, but other than that, it's not getting worse."

"It's not getting worse?"

She shakes her head. "No. You've just been in a holding pattern."

"So, what . . . I mean, you said . . ." She said there were a couple of things we could do, but I don't even want to say that out loud, because I can feel it already. The hope stirring inside me, the hope I've done everything I can to tamp down. It's swelling into a wave, threatening to take over.

"Right," she says. "There are a couple of things we can do. The first is riskier, but it could give you full use of your arm back. It's a surgery. Now, I need to be honest with you. If it doesn't work, it could make it worse."

I feel like the wind has been knocked out of me. "You said . . . I mean, I could . . . My shoulder could work again?"

"Yes." She nods. "But if it doesn't work, then you could lose some of your mobility. The reason I need to tell you that is because I know with athletes, some of them decide that the risk is too great. Some of them want to play overseas, that kind of thing."

I know what she means. She's saying that if the surgery doesn't work, and I get worse, I might lose my chance to play in a smaller market, like Japan or something like that. But fuck Japan. I never wanted to play there anyway, and it's not like anyone from overseas ever made any effort to contact me.

I put my hand up, stopping her from going on.

"I don't need to hear the second option," I say. "I want the surgery."

She starts talking about plans and schedules, and a bunch of stuff I'm going to have to consider, like recovery time and things like that. But I'm not hearing any of it. Because all I can think about is telling Harper.

Harper

I'm so focused that when it's my turn, I don't hear them call my name. The girl next to me, this really bratty-looking brunette who's wearing hot pink leg warmers (wtf?), has to poke me in the side until I pull my headphones out.

"Um, I think they're calling your name," she says, rolling her eyes. "Like, you have to pay attention, you know?"

"Thanks," I say, deciding not to let her bad attitude rattle me.

I convinced myself not to be scared, that the people I'm auditioning for are just people, that they'll be nice, that it won't be like one of those movies where you walk in and everyone's really dressed up and intimidating and they make you feel like a jerk.

But it's exactly like a movie.

Well, not exactly.

The choreography admissions people are friendly enough, but they *are* intimidating. I recognize them immediately. Katie Fox, Reginald Perry, and April Dewan. They're all choreographers who've done music videos, Broadway shows, you name it. Right away my palms start sweating, and I wipe them on my dance tights, and then immediately regret it. I already don't have the right outfit, and now I'm wrecking it even more.

"Hi, Harper," Katie says, looking down at the list in front of her. "What are you going to be doing for us today?"

"I'm going to be doing a piece to 'Smooth Criminal' by Michael Jackson." I watch their eyes to see if there's any reaction, if they think it's a cheesy song, or not classic enough, or if maybe they like the idea that I've chosen something a little riskier.

"Okay," Reginald says. His smile is friendly, but it doesn't give anything away. "Whenever you're ready."

I take a moment to calm my breathing, and to remind myself that whatever happens, I'll be okay. But, damn, I want this so freaking bad.

I nod to the girl in the corner who's in charge of the music, and the first bars of the song come echoing through the room. The music is louder than I expected, which I like. I love when the music reverberates through my body, taking over so that I don't have to think about anything except the beat.

I know they're not judging me on my dancing. I'm here for the choreography program, which means I need to know how to put a dance together and teach it, not be the best technically. But I also know that how I dance my piece is going to be a factor in how good they think my choreography is. If I'm a big mess, then they're not going to be able to see how good my dance is.

I focus as best as I can on the moves, letting myself get lost in the music. For the first few steps I can feel myself being timid. I'm too aware of the three people watching me, and an inventory of their impressive qualifications is rolling through my head. I'm imagining them making up dances for Britney, for Beyoncé, for Katy Perry, and I'm not just letting go. I can't stop worrying about what they must think of me.

But then I tell myself to forget all that. Instead I listen for the beats, feel them pulse through my body. This is what I love about dance. Even though I'm not the best dancer, I love the way my body feels when I'm doing it. I love the way the movements make you feel like you're free, like you're floating.

When the song ends, I realize that after those first few steps, I've heard every single note of it, that I've been in the moment with every bar, every lyric, every beat. At the same time I can't remember exactly what I did. It's like my body just took over and did what it was always meant to.

"Thanks, Harper," the three of them say, writing on their sheets.

"You're welcome," I say. "Thanks for letting me audition for you."

When I walk out of the room, I'm sweaty and smiling, and

I feel happy and rejuvenated. I don't even mind the fact that the other girls are giving me looks, sizing me up and trying to figure out if I've stolen a spot that could have been theirs. It doesn't bother me, because these aren't the kind of girls who end up in the dance program anyway. When I went to visit earlier this year, everyone was nice and friendly and eager to help.

I walk outside, and the sun is shining, and I feel better than I have in a while. I think about calling my mom, or texting Anna to tell them how well it went. But then I decide to hold it in for just a little bit longer. I want it to be my secret for a few more moments. I don't want to tell anyone else.

Yes, you do, a voice whispers. *You want to tell Penn.*

I try to tell myself it's not true.

But I know deep down that it is. The only person I want to tell is Penn.

Penn

I have to find her.

I need to get to her.

But I don't know where she is. I know she's not at school. I drive by her house, but her car isn't in the driveway. I wish I could remember where that stupid audition was, but I'm not sure if she ever even told me. And if she did and I can't remember, well, then, no wonder she hates me. It's just another reason I was a completely shitty boyfriend.

I don't realize where I'm going until I pull up in front of the dance studio. And there it is. Her car, in the parking lot. She must be done with her audition. She must be in the studio.

I cut the engine and rush inside. Her mom's there, teaching that crazy couple, the one who was here that first day.

"You're stepping on my feet!" the girl screeches. "Jeremy, stop it! What are you trying to do, break my toes? You weigh, like, two hundred pounds!"

"Okay," Harper's mom says, rubbing her temples. "Maybe we should take a small break."

She tries to smile, but I can tell she's completely annoyed with the both of them. And I don't blame her. They're acting like absolute babies.

"Hi," I say. "Sorry to interrupt."

"Penn," Harper's mom says, seemingly startled. "What are you doing here?"

"Is Harper here?"

Her mom shakes her head. "No."

"No?"

"No. She's at her audition."

"But her car's in the parking lot."

"We switched cars this morning," her mom says. "She took mine because she's been having some trouble with hers, and she wanted to make sure nothing got in the way of her audition."

"Oh." I hate that I don't know this. I hate that I don't know Harper was having car trouble and that I wasn't there to help her. I take a deep breath. "Do you know where her audition is? I kind of need to talk to her."

Her mom shakes her head again. "I really don't think that's a good idea. Harper needs to focus on what she's doing."

"Oh, I'm not going to barge in or anything." I'm not sure if I'm going to or not, actually. I mean, I intend on waiting in the parking lot, but now that I've made this decision, now that I've decided I need to talk to Harper, then I need to talk to Harper. "I'm just going to wait until she's done."

Harper's mom shakes her head. "I don't think it's a good idea, Penn."

"Please," I say, and I can hear the desperation in my voice. "I just . . . I need to talk to her, and she's not . . . I need to talk to her in person."

"Oh, tell him," the girl dance student, Kaitlyn or whatever, says. "He's obviously in love."

The guy sort of laughs, but Kaitlyn gives him a soft punch on the shoulder. "Don't you dare make fun of him! He's in love. He's willing to do things for the woman he loves, unlike you."

"Whaddya call this?" the guy asks. "I'm here, aren't I? I'm doing this stupid dance for you!"

"Please," I say to Harper's mom, not even caring that the guy is basically calling me a wimp. I kind of deserve it for telling him to get some balls when I first met him. "I need to see her. I won't barge in on her audition, I swear."

Harper's mom sighs. I can tell she doesn't want to tell me. I try to convince myself it's not the end of the world, that I'll just wait until Harper's done, until she's home, and then I'll be able to talk to her.

But at the last second Harper's mom must take pity on me, because before I know what's happening, she says, "It's the Crowne Plaza in Natick."

I'm running out the door before she even finishes her sentence. "Thank you," I call over my shoulder. "Thank you."

Harper

I'm sitting in the hotel restaurant eating a piece of chocolate cake when Penn comes barging into the lobby looking like a man possessed. I watch, dumbfounded, as he sits down on one of the couches in the check-in area, his leg moving up and down like he can't sit still.

What the hell is he doing here? Is he here to see me? No. It makes no sense. Why would he be here to see me? I watch him for a moment, and I feel a whirlwind of emotion stirring up inside me, and I expect it to turn into a hurricane, to overtake me, but it doesn't. It just sort of moves through my body like a dust storm, before settling in my stomach and staying there.

He looks gorgeous, his dark hair flopping over his forehead the way it does, his eyes dark and intense the way they always are. He pulls out his phone and texts someone.

I remember that my phone is off, and I pull it out and turn it on.

The texts pop up right away.

At an appointment with another doctor. I miss you. A lot.

And then, a second later, the one he just sent.

I'm in the lobby. I'll wait for you.

He looks up at that moment, almost like he knows I'm watching him. And then he gets up and walks over to me. I stand up.

"Hey," he says softly. He shoves his hands into his pockets and gives me a half smile.

"What are you doing here?" I blurt.

"I came to see you."

"How did you know I was here?"

"Your mom told me."

"You talked to my *mom*?"

"Yeah. I thought you might have been at the studio, so I went there, and she told me."

I don't know if I want to kiss her or kill her. Why would she tell him where I am? Am I happy he's here? I don't know.

"You're eating chocolate cake?" he asks.

"Yes." Chocolate cake is Penn's favorite. I know I should offer him some, but I don't.

"How did the audition go?" he asks.

"Fine." I don't want to tell him how it went. I don't want to tell him how well it went, how amazing I felt afterward, and how not being able to share it with him was the only thing that kept the moment from being perfect.

"Good." He looks at me, and then takes a step toward me, wrapping his arms around my waist. "God, Harper," he says into my ear. "I missed you so much."

His breath tickles my skin, and I break into goose bumps. "Penn," I say quietly, and use every ounce of my self-control to force myself to take a step back. "Why are you here?"

"I went to another doctor," he says. "Dr. Marzetti."

I don't say anything.

"Harper, she thinks she can fix my shoulder."

I inhale sharply. "She can?"

He nods. "It's not a definite, but she's the first one who even thinks there's a chance."

He reaches for me again, and this time, when his arms encircle me and pull me into his chest, I don't resist. I lean into him. He feels so good and . . . I love him. It's the first time the word has entered my mind, and it's shocking and weird to feel like I love him. But I do. I really do love him.

"Can we get out of here?" he murmurs into my hair. "Can we leave? Because I really want to talk to you."

I open my mouth to say yes. But then I stop myself. I remember how it felt these past three weeks, how my heart broke every time I passed by him in the hall, how every time I looked at my phone and saw he hadn't texted me, I died a little inside.

I pull back. "Penn," I say. "You can't . . . I mean, we can't just pretend like nothing happened."

"No, I know," he says. "I don't want to pretend anymore, Harper. I want to talk about things."

I look into his eyes, trying to figure out if he means it. He's not lying to me—at least, not intentionally. I know he thinks he means what he's saying. But Penn can't just switch things on and off, depending on his mood of the moment. What's going to happen when he gets bad news from this doctor? Or when he comes out of surgery and finds out he can't play the way he used to? What happens when I ask him about his family again, and he completely shuts down? Then what?

I shake my head.

"Penn," I say. "I'm sorry. I can't."

And then I turn around and run.

And that's how I end up crying in the bathroom of the Crowne Plaza in Natick, my broken heart in pieces all around me.

Penn

This is how it ends:

With me standing here alone in the restaurant of the hotel while Harper runs away from me.

I don't understand.

She wanted me to let her in.

And now that I'm finally ready, she's running.

After that things go back to normal.

I go to school.

I come home.

My dad disappears and reappears. I see Harper every day at school, and every day it starts to hurt a little bit less.

I schedule my surgery with Dr. Marzetti. By the end of

the summer, I'll know if the surgery has worked. I get in touch with some of the recruiters from schools that lost interest after I got hurt. Surprisingly, they're happy to hear from me, and excited to know that I might soon be back to full strength.

I start to get back to the gym, and even do a couple of workouts with the baseball team. It's after one of these work-outs that I run into Jackson. He's at his car, loading his stuff into his trunk.

I don't realize I was following him until I'm standing right behind him.

He slams the trunk shut and turns around. When he sees me, he holds his hands up. "Whoa, whoa, whoa," he says, like he's surrendering. "If you want to start something, don't do it on school property. If I get written up one more time, Coach is going to have a hissy fit."

"I don't want to fight you." I take in a deep breath and let it out slowly. "I wanted to thank you."

He stops and looks at me skeptically. "Thank me? For what?"

"For getting me that doctor's appointment."

He shakes his head. "You're kidding me, right?"

"No."

"Dude, you came to my house a few weeks ago looking like you wanted to beat my ass because I made you that appoint-ment."

"I know." I look up at him. "I was wrong for the way I treated you." As I'm saying it, I realize I'm talking about more than just what happened that day at his house. I'm talking about what happened after the accident, about how I just completely shut him out after I got hurt. Of course it wasn't Jackson's fault. And I knew that.

Jackson stands there for a long moment, and then nods. "What made you change your mind?"

I shrug. "After I went to that appointment, it made me realize that bad news isn't the end of the world. There's always a chance for something better."

He nods. "And Harper?"

I'm surprised he noticed she was a part of it. But when I think about it, I'm really not that surprised. I mean, he's my best friend. "Harper changed my mind too," I say. "She was a big part of it."

"But you're not together?"

I shake my head. "She doesn't . . . It was too late."

Jackson shakes his head and twirls his key ring around his finger the way I've seen him do a million times before. "It's never too late, Mattingly." He grins and gets into the car. "If you want her, get her."

And then he slams the door and drives away.

Harper

Here's what happens:

Anna gets over Nico and develops this major crush on a guy named Howard Pierce. He's a junior, and she spends tons of time talking about how great a singer he is, and how he's this untapped talent who's going to do big things.

The weather gets hotter, and everyone starts amping up for graduation. No one can sit still in class, and school becomes an excruciating exercise in waiting and anticipation.

It's humid and muggy the day I get my acceptance letter for the choreography program at Ballard. I run into the house, screaming and yelling as I wave the letter in the air like a crazy person. My mom hugs me close and tells me how proud she is of me.

She never asked me about that day at my audition, at least

not the part about Penn. And I never asked her why she told him where I was, or what he said to her to get her to tell him. The irony isn't lost on me. This whole time I was pushing Penn to talk about how he felt, telling him it was important not to keep things buried inside, and yet I refuse to talk about my breakup with anyone.

It's the last week of school and I'm standing at my locker before class.

Suddenly there's a tap on my shoulder.

I turn around.

My heart drops into my stomach.

It's the school nurse.

"Well, well, well," she says, giving me a smile. "Harper Fairbanks. We finally come face-to-face."

I swallow, not sure what to say. "I'm sorry," I say finally, pasting an innocent expression on my face. "Do I know you?"

"Oh, don't pretend like you don't know who I am," she says. "I'm the school nurse. And you, my dear, are overdue for your physical. I really have no idea how you managed to escape my clutches for so long."

She holds up her clipboard, where she's printed out my yearbook picture from last year. Wow. Talk about psycho.

I sigh. "Listen," I say. "I don't—"

"Well, you have to." She cuts me off.

And then, suddenly, out of nowhere, a voice comes through the crowd. "Harper! There you are!"

I turn around. Penn.

My heart clenches when I see him, and the fact that he's saying my name makes my pulse race.

"Harper," he says urgently. "Where the hell have you been? We have to get out of here!"

"What?" I'm confused.

He winks at me, and then I realize what he's doing. He's trying to get me out of this. "We're late for our interviews."

"Oh, right!" I say. "Our interviews!"

"What interviews?" the nurse demands.

Penn gives her a reassuring smile. "We have interviews with a Yale recruiter," he says. "We're going to be the first students in the history of this school to even get into Yale. Isn't that exciting? We're going to be in the newspaper."

She narrows her eyes. "But Harper needs to come with me to the—"

"We have to go! The principal knows all about it. He'll tell you."

Penn starts hustling me down the hall, leaving the nurse standing there, staring after us in bewilderment. I can tell she doesn't really believe us, but she doesn't know for sure.

"Thanks," I say shyly once we're safely out of sight and standing by the cafeteria doors.

"You're welcome."

This is the part where he should turn and walk away, but he doesn't. Instead he just stands there, looking at me.

"You do know that she's probably going to just try to find me tomorrow, right?" I ask.

He shrugs. "You've avoided her this long. You'll figure something out." He grins, that same little grin that made me fall in love with him. It makes me sad that it isn't mine to love anymore.

"Yeah." I know I should turn to go, but I can't. It's like my feet are rooted in one spot.

"You look good, Harper."

"I got into the choreography program," I blurt, because I don't know what else to say, and I have to say something, because if I don't, I'm afraid he's going to turn around and walk away.

"You did? That's amazing. Congratulations."

"Thanks."

"I might be going to Duke, or UNC."

I swallow, then ask the question anyway. "Baseball?"

"We'll see. I have my surgery right after graduation."

"That's awesome, Penn. I'm really happy for you."

"Thanks."

The bell rings then, and everyone starts to move toward their classrooms. The hall is quiet and silent now, and yet we still stand there, acting like we're not supposed to be in class, acting like it's not strange that we're talking.

"Harper," he says. "I still miss you. I think about you every day."

I want to say it back. But I can't do it. I can't let him back in again. "Take care of yourself, Penn." I turn around before he can see the tears starting to run down my cheeks.

But he calls my name. "Harper?"

I turn around.

"My dad's an alcoholic. That's why you've never been to my house. My mom and my brother act like it's not happening, that when he disappears, he's just on some business trip or something and not out on a bender."

I suck in a breath. "I'm sorry," I say. "I had no idea—"

But he cuts me off. He crosses the space between us in two long strides, until he's so close to me, it hurts. "You once told me," he says, "that I needed to take a chance. That I needed to let you in. And I did, Harper. It took me longer than I wanted it to take, and I'm still working on it. But I went to the doctor, and I just told you about my family. I'm a work in progress." His eyes are burning that intense, sexy look that he always gets when he's being sincere about something. "And now I'm asking you to take a chance on me."

He runs his hands up my arms, and a little shiver slides up and down my spine.

"Penn," I say. "You hurt me so bad. You have no idea how much I cried and how much I missed you."

He pulls me close, and this time I let him.

I close my eyes and inhale his scent—Axe body wash, peppermint, and laundry soap. I missed him so much.

"Take a chance on me, Harper," he says. "And I'll never hurt you again."

I know it's a promise he can't really keep. No one can promise they're never going to hurt you. But I know he's being sincere. I know he's trying. He's asking me to take a chance on him, the way I asked him to take a chance on me, and on us.

And the truth is, I want to. I want to be with him.

He stands there in the empty hall with me, just holding me, rubbing my back and letting the emotions wash over us.

Finally I pull back. "Okay," I say. "Okay, I'll take a chance."

He smiles and takes my hand. Then he leans in close and whispers into my ear, "You want to get out of here?"

I smile. "Always."

And then he's leading me through the halls, and past the boys' locker room, and out the side entrance. The air is warm, and the sun feels good on my face.

"Where should we go?" he asks once we have our seat belts on.

I smile at him. "Surprise me."

He puts the car into reverse and pulls out of the parking lot and onto the main road. I think about the first day we met, how we drove out of this same parking lot and I had no idea where we were going. But that's how it is with the best journeys, I decide. You never know where you're going to end up until you're there.

I roll down the window and let the warm summer breeze blow through my hair. Our journey might be just beginning, but I'm already right where I'm supposed to be.

Check out this excerpt from Lauren's novel

THE THING ABOUT
THE TRUTH!

the thing about
the truth

LAUREN BARNHOLDT

author of *two-way street* and *sometimes it happens*

The Aftermath

Office of the Superintendent, 11:26 a.m.

Kelsey

I am in so much trouble. So, so, so much trouble. Seriously, I cannot even begin to *imagine* the kind of trouble I'm in. It's the kind of trouble you hope you're never going to be in, the kind of trouble you hear people talk about, and you go, *"Wow, what an idiot. I'm glad I'm never going to be in that kind of trouble."*

I'm probably going to get kicked out of school. My second school in three months. What will happen to me then? Where will I even go? The last school I got kicked out of was Concordia Prep, a private school, so of course I got put into public school. But where do you go when you get kicked out of public school? Reform school or something?

God, that would be horrible. I could never last at a reform

school. I have a pink Kate Spade purse, for God's sake. I got it at the Kate Spade outlet, but still. Reform school would eat me alive. I'd be like one of those girls on those shows on Spike TV, where they take the teen troublemakers and put them in jail for a day to show them where they're headed, and they all break down and start crying and completely lose their shit.

I shift in my chair and look at the clock: 11:27. The meeting with the superintendent, Dr. Ostrander, is supposed to start in three minutes, and Isaac still isn't here. Not that I'm surprised. Isaac is never on time to anything.

The clock's hand ticks over to 11:28, and I start to think that maybe he's not coming. That maybe somehow his dad got him out of it, and that I'm going to be left dealing with this mess on my own.

But then the door to the office opens, and Isaac walks in. His dark eyes scan the room, moving over the secretary, taking in the closed door that leads to Dr. Ostrander's office, and then finally landing on me. Without even talking to the secretary or telling anyone he's there, he walks over and plops himself down in the chair two down from me.

He doesn't say anything, just keeps his gaze facing forward. I sneak a look at him out of the corner of my eye. He's wearing pressed khaki pants, a light blue button-down shirt, and a red-and-blue tie. His black shoes are perfectly shined, his hair freshly gelled. He looks put together, in control, and, as always, completely gorgeous. There's a slight scowl on his face, but it only serves to make him look more in charge of the situation, like he can't believe what a total waste of time this whole thing is.

He turns to look at me, and when he does, he catches *me* looking at *him,* and my heart stops.

"Hey," I say. I'm not sure if we're talking, but the word is out of my mouth before I can stop it.

"Hey." His tone is clipped. He's still mad at me for what happened, still hurt, still upset. Still probably doesn't want to give me another chance.

"I was starting to think you weren't going to come," I say. It's a lame thing to say, but I'm desperate to keep the conversation going.

"Why wouldn't I come?" He looks like he thinks I'm crazy for doubting he would show up.

"I don't know. I thought maybe your dad . . ."

He rolls his eyes and looks away.

"Anyway," I say, "I'm glad you're here."

He doesn't reply, just pulls his cell phone out of his pocket. His fingers move over the screen, checking his texts, reading something, typing a reply. I wonder who he's texting with. Marina? Doubtful, but honestly, at this point, nothing would surprise me.

"Mr. Brandano, Ms. Romano?" the secretary says. "Dr. Ostrander will see you now." I take a deep breath and stand up. I smooth my skirt, a simple black pencil skirt chosen in an effort to make me look mature and trustworthy.

"Here we go," I say to Isaac, and flash him a smile. It's

an attempt to show that we're in this together, that we're both heading into the lion's den, but that maybe we can be okay if we just depend on each other.

But Isaac doesn't say anything. He just turns on the heel of his superexpensive, supershiny black shoe and walks toward Dr. Ostrander's office door. I stand there for a moment, blinking back the tears that are threatening to spill down my cheeks.

I'm upset because Isaac won't talk to me, but mostly I'm upset because I know that this whole thing is my fault. The reason we might get kicked out of school. The reason everything's so completely screwed up. And most of all, the reason we broke up. The reason I've probably lost him forever.

I've spent so many hours thinking about it, going over it again and again in my mind. If I start doing that now, I'll drive myself crazy, letting my thoughts become a tangled mess. And I need to keep my mind clear for this meeting. So I wipe at my eyes with the back of my hand and then force myself to head into Dr. Ostrander's office.

Before

Kelsey

So, my first day at Concordia Public is definitely not off to a great start. First, I spilled orange juice all over the skirt I was wearing. Which was bullshit, since (a) I don't usually even eat breakfast, and (b) I don't even really like orange juice. But this morning when I came downstairs, my dad insisted that I "get something in my stomach" so that I would have energy for my first day at my new school. So I choked down a piece of dry toast and a glass of orange juice, mostly just to please him (that's a whole other story—the doing it just to please him part), and then I spilled it on my skirt. And I had no time to change before the bus came.

Which was another thing. The bus. Riding the bus, in case

you don't know, really sucks. But I don't have a license yet (I'm seventeen, but I've failed my driver's test twice—fingers crossed, though, for my next try!), and there was no way my parents were going to give me a ride to school. They were trying to teach me a lesson, I think. Which makes no sense. How was not driving me to school causing me to learn a lesson? I already learned my lesson when I got kicked out of my old school.

Hopefully, I'll be able to make some new friends quickly. New friends who won't mind picking me up in the morning.

But so far, the prospects at Concordia Public are not looking very promising.

I'm sitting in the guidance office, waiting to have a meeting with my guidance counselor so I can get my schedule and locker combination, and no one here looks even remotely like potential new friend material. I mean, the girl sitting next to me has pink hair and five piercings in each ear. Which is fine. I might be preppy, but I'm not, like, *discriminatory* or anything.

I can be friends with people who have piercings. Not that I ever really have before, but I have nothing against it. I love piercings. I have two in each ear, even. But it's the girl's bag that's the real problem. It's a camouflage print. Which again, whatever. Not my style, but fine. But what *isn't* fine is the patch that's sewn on the front. It says KILL ALL PREPS.

I might not be prejudiced, but she definitely is. I quickly move my Prada shoes (borrowed from my friend Rielle) farther under my chair.

The irony of the whole thing is that I kind of feel the same way she does. Preps do kind of suck. But at my old school, Concordia Prep, everyone was preppy. (Haha, preps at a prep school, big surprise, right?)

Anyway, I was a scholarship student, so I was always trying to make sure I fit in. And that meant having Kate Spade purses and Prada shoes. Even when I couldn't afford it, I would—

The door to the office opens and a boy walks in. Dark blond hair. Sparkling white sneakers. Perfectly faded jeans. He walks with a swagger, the kind that comes from years of being confident. You can't teach a walk like that. Trust me, I've tried to cultivate one. It's impossible.

I make a mental note to stay away from him. He's probably the most popular guy in school, the kind who's mean to everyone, the kind who, for some inexplicable reason, has all the girls wanting him. Why are girls like that, anyway? They're always falling for the jerks. Which is ridiculous. Not that I don't have experience when it comes to that kind of thing.

I mean, I wouldn't be here if I hadn't fallen in love with a jerk. A jerk is the reason I got kicked out of my old school.

But I've learned my lesson.

I look over at the girl next to me, and she's practically falling out of her chair, that's how bad she wants this guy. Poor thing. She doesn't know what she's in for. And besides, I thought she hated all preps. I guess it doesn't apply to hot male preps with perfect hair and perfect—

Mr. Popular is speaking.

"Hello," he says to the secretary, leaning over the desk. "I'm Isaac Brandano. It's my first day, and I was told to come to the office and pick up my schedule."

I almost choke on the peppermint latte I'm drinking. It's this guy's first day? And he's walking like *that*?

"Yes, Mr. Brandano," the secretary says, all friendly. She gives him a smile. When I came in here, she totally scowled at me and acted like I was making her day into a big debacle. "Here you go." She hands him a schedule. What, he doesn't have to sit here and take a meeting with his guidance counselor like everyone else?

Ohmigod. Probably only the rejects who got kicked out of their old schools need to have meetings with their guidance counselors. How humiliating.

Mr. Popular thanks her, then turns toward the door, his eyes running down over his schedule. He frowns slightly, probably because he can't believe they would dare to put him in math or something.

He looks up, his eyes meeting mine. His are dark and slightly brooding, the color of chocolate, and I feel my heart skip a beat. I mean, I'm only human.

"Hey," he says.

"Hi," the girl next to me says, totally butting in.

"Do either of you know where room 107 is?" He smiles, showing perfect white teeth. Real white. Not the kind of white that comes from using those whitening strips or spending hundreds of dollars at the dentist. Rielle has that kind of teeth, along with tons of other girls at Concordia Prep.

"No," I say firmly. I've gotten ahold of my hormones, so I take another sip of my latte and then turn back to the book I'm reading.

"No?" He sounds a little incredulous. I guess he's surprised that I don't want to help him. Obviously, he doesn't know that I'm new and thinks I'm just being a bitch. Which I kind of like. That he thinks I'm being a bitch, I mean. It's sort of amusing.

"No," I repeat.

"I do," the pink-haired girl offers. "I know where it is."

But Isaac Brandano isn't paying attention to her. He's still looking at me. The only reason I've even remembered his name is because he has the same last name as our state senator, John Bran— Oh. My. God. No freakin' way. Isaac Brandano is our state senator's son!

There was all this talk on the news last night about how John Brandano was going to be sending his son to public school in order to prove that a public school education is just as good as a private school one. Of course, I doubt that's really true. I mean, public school is—

"You don't know where room 107 is?" Isaac Brandano's asking me. "You have no idea?" Now his incredulousness makes even more sense. I mean, not only is he gorgeous, but he's a senator's son. Which means he's used to people doing whatever he wants and falling all over themselves to help him. Now I'm doubly happy that he thinks I'm messing with him.

"No," I say simply. "Sorry, I don't. But I suppose that you expect me to find out for you."

"No." He shakes his head. "I don't expect that, I just . . ." He looks shocked that someone would be mean to him, and for a second I feel bad. I mean, I *am* being a bitch. And if it were anyone else, I would tell him that I'm new and that's the reason I can't show him where the room is. And let's face it, I'm a little on edge today, which is definitely affecting my mood.

I can't feel too bad, though, because honestly? Probably no one's ever been mean to him in his life. Probably he's used to just smiling at people and having them fall in love with him and do whatever he wants, like he just did with the secretary.

I know his type. I've handled his type. I'm at this stupid school because of his type.

"I'm sorry," Isaac says. He's still looking at me, and he shakes his head again like he doesn't know what just happened, like he wants to start again. "I just—"

"I can show you where the room is," the girl next to me says. She stands up and starts to gather up her bag.

"There you go," I say. "See? It all worked out." I go back to reading my book. Honestly, now I just want the both of them to go away. I need to focus on my meeting and making a good impression on my guidance counselor. Now that I've been kicked out of one of the best prep schools in the country, my college recommendations are going to be doubly important.

Isaac follows the pink-haired girl out into the hallway. Good riddance.

"Ms. Romano?" the secretary asks. Now that Isaac and his good looks have disappeared out the door, she's back to being all frosty. "Mr. Lawler will see you now."

"Thanks." I put my book back in my bag. And then I step into my guidance counselor's office, ready to make a good impression and take the first step toward getting my future back on track.

Before

Isaac

This school is completely fucked up. Seriously, what the hell is going on? Is this how public school is going to be? People just being *mean* to you for no reason? That girl in the guidance office was just . . . I don't know.

I guess I expected people to be a little rude because of who my dad is. At my old school I didn't have to worry about that, since no one really gave a shit. Everyone's parents were important. In fact, there were some kids who had celebrity parents.

But a lot of people get all weird about it. There are people, like that secretary back there, who fall all over themselves trying to be nice to you. And then there are people who go out of their way to show you that they're not going to give you any special treatment. So I knew public school would be different, but I didn't expect to encounter it during my first minute here.

I knew I shouldn't have worn my new sneakers today. Way too flashy.

"So, are you, like, a transfer?" The girl showing me to my homeroom is blabbering on and on, but I haven't been listening to her because I've been distracted, thinking about that girl in the office.

"Yeah," I say, looking around the hallway. "I'm a transfer." Obviously, she hasn't heard about me. Which is to be expected. This whole starting public school thing was a little sudden. My dad's spinning it so that it seems as if he's sending me to public school to make a statement about education or some shit. But the reality is I got kicked out of my last school, and I'm sort of at the end of the line when it comes to private schools. It was either here, or boarding school overseas. And when that possibility came up, I pitched a fit.

The numbers on the rooms are going down as we walk: 119, 117, 115. . . . Hell, if I had known it was going to be this easy to find my homeroom, I never would have even asked for help.

"Where'd you transfer from?" the girl's asking.

"Hotchmann," I say. She looks at me blankly, so I add, "It's a boarding school in New York City."

Her eyes widen. "Wow," she says. "How'd you end up here?"

"My dad thought it would be a good idea."

She nods. She still has no idea who I am, although that's probably going to change soon.

We're in front of the room now. "So, here we are," she says, giving me a bright smile.

I peek inside. The desks are filled with kids sitting, chatting with friends, looking through their bags, texting on their cell phones. There's no teacher in there yet, which is good. The last thing I need is to walk in and have some teacher make a big production out of things. I hate big productions. My life has been an endless string of big productions, and I'm over it.

I turn back to the girl with pink hair.

"Thanks for walking me," I say. "What's your name?"

"Melissa."

"Well, thanks, Melissa." I give her a smile and then head into the classroom. No one looks at me, and obviously I don't have any friends to sit with, so I pick a seat in the middle of the room, deciding that sitting not too close to the back and not too close to the front is a good idea.

As soon as I'm in my chair, the guy in front of me turns around and glares at me. Jesus Christ. People really are not too friendly around here. I might have to go public with this, start some kind of blog or some shit. Tell everyone that public schools really are subpar, that the people here are dangerous. Seriously, the first time I see a knife, I'm writing an exposé.

"That seat's taken," the dude ahead of me says.

"Oh, really?" I ask. "Because it doesn't look like anyone's sitting here." I'm figuring this place is kind of like prison. You have to make sure that you stand up for yourself right off the bat; otherwise these pricks will walk all over you. I put my notebook on the desk, not really able to believe that I'm staking out my territory in a suburban public school homeroom.

He narrows his eyes at me. "Who are you?" he demands.

"Isaac," I say, deciding it's best to leave my last name out of it.

"You're new?"

"Yeah."

He nods like he can accept this. "What do you play?"

"What do I play?"

"Yeah."

"Sports or women?"

He considers. "Either."

"Lacrosse and basketball."

He nods again, like this, too, is acceptable. "And what about girls?"

"I play them." It's true. I do play them. Not in a completely jerky way. I just like to have fun. And something tells me this dude will appreciate that.

"I'm Marshall." I'm not sure if that's his first name or his last, but I reach out and shake the hand that he's offering. "You should stick with me," he says. "I'll show you around."

I think about it. He looks kind of like a jock meathead, but that's probably not the worst crowd to fall in with. Not to mention that he's the first person who's actually been nice to me.

Actually, no. That's not true. Melissa or whatever her name

is was nice to me. Which means that girl in the office was an exception to the rule.

Still. Beggars can't be choosers.

"Cool," I say to Marshall. And just like that, I might have my first friend.